DRAGON MASTERS

WAKING THE RAINBOW DRAGON

BY

TRACEY WEST

ILLUSTRATED BY

DAMIEN JONES

SCHOLASTIC INC.

DRAGON MASTERS

Read All the Adventures

1. DRAGON MASTERS — RISE OF THE EARTH DRAGON
2. DRAGON MASTERS — SAVING THE SUN DRAGON
3. DRAGON MASTERS — SECRET OF THE WATER DRAGON
4. DRAGON MASTERS — POWER OF THE FIRE DRAGON
5. DRAGON MASTERS — SONG OF THE POISON DRAGON
6. DRAGON MASTERS — FLIGHT OF THE MOON DRAGON
7. DRAGON MASTERS — SEARCH FOR THE LIGHTNING DRAGON
8. DRAGON MASTERS — ROAR OF THE THUNDER DRAGON
9. DRAGON MASTERS — CHILL OF THE ICE DRAGON
10. DRAGON MASTERS — WAKING THE RAINBOW DRAGON
11. DRAGON MASTERS — SHINE OF THE SILVER DRAGON

More books coming soon!

TABLE OF CONTENTS

FOR TRISTAN AND CORA,

who were chosen by the Dragon Stone. —TW

Text copyright © 2018 by Tracey West
Interior illustrations copyright © 2018 Scholastic Inc.

Library of Congress Cataloging-in-Publication Data
Names: West, Tracey, 1965- author. Jones, Damien, illustrator. West, Tracey, 1965- Dragon Masters; 10.
Title: Waking the rainbow dragon/by Tracey West; illustrated by Damien Jones.
Description: First edition. New York, NY: Branches/Scholastic Inc., 2018. Series: Dragon masters; 10
Summary: Drake has a dream about a new dragon that is somehow trapped in a cave, so Drake, Ana, and their two dragons set off to find the Rainbow Dragon's dragon master, Obi, and together they must rescue Rainbow dragon, Dayo, from Kwaku, a giant spider, who spins a deadly web.
Identifiers: LCCN 2017037057 ISBN 9781338169898 (pbk.) ISBN 9781338169904 (hardcover)
Subjects: LCSH: Dragons—Juvenile fiction. Magic—Juvenile fiction. Spiders—Juvenile fiction. Adventure stories. CYAC: Dragons—Fiction. Magic—Fiction. Spiders—Fiction. Adventure and adventurers—Fiction.
Classification: LCC PZ7.W51937 Wak 2018 DDC 813.54 [Fic] —dc23 LC record available at https://lccn.loc.gov/2017037057

10 9 8 7 6 5 4 3 2 1   18 19 20 21 22

Printed in China   38
First edition, July 2018
Illustrated by Damien Jones
Edited by Katie Carella
Book design by Jessica Meltzer

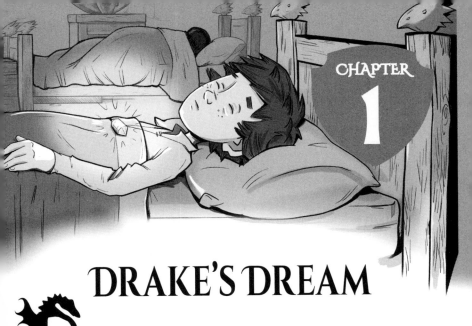

DRAKE'S DREAM

Drake was dreaming about a dragon.

Months before, Drake had been chosen to be a Dragon Master. He had been taken from his home and brought to King Roland's castle. There, he had learned that dragons were real.

Drake had been given his own dragon, Worm, a powerful Earth Dragon. Now they lived in the castle with the other Dragon Masters and their dragons: Kepri, a Sun Dragon; Shu, a Water Dragon; Vulcan, a Fire Dragon; and Zera, a Poison Dragon.

He had met other dragons during his adventures: Wati, a Moon Dragon; Lalo, a Lightning Dragon; Neru, a Thunder Dragon; and Frost, an Ice Dragon.

Drake dreamed about these dragons all the time. But the dragon in *this* dream was different.

She had a long body, like a snake's. Her scales shimmered with rows of stripes in different colors — red, orange, yellow, green, blue, and purple. Just like a rainbow.

It was a beautiful dream. The Rainbow Dragon flew across a blue sky. Her body curved like a rainbow. White clouds appeared and rain began to fall.

But then the rain stopped. The earth dried up. The scene changed to a dark cave. The Rainbow Dragon was curled up there. She looked frightened. A shadowy figure came toward her . . .

Drake jolted awake. His best friend, Bo, sat up across the room.

"Are you okay, Drake?" Bo asked.

"Yes," Drake replied. "I just had a dream. It felt so real. It was about a dragon."

"Are you sure it was a dream?" Bo asked. "Your Dragon Stone is glowing. Maybe Worm was trying to tell you something."

Drake looked down at the green stone that hung from a chain around his neck. Every Dragon Master wore one. It allowed them to connect with their dragons.

"You might be right, Bo!" Drake said. He jumped out of bed and quickly got dressed. "I'll find out! See you at breakfast!"

Drake ran downstairs. He raced through the underground Training Room to the caves where the dragons slept. He found Worm waiting for him.

"Worm, did you send me that dream? The dream about the Rainbow Dragon?" Drake asked.

Worm nodded. Drake's Dragon Stone glowed again. He heard Worm's voice inside his head.

Yes, Worm said. *The Rainbow Dragon needs our help!*

CHAPTER 2

THE POWER OF RAIN

Where is the Rainbow Dragon?" Drake asked.

Worm shook his head. *I do not know.*

Drake frowned. "Griffith will know how to find her," he said.

Drake ran upstairs to the dining room. Griffith, the wizard who taught them, was there. He was eating breakfast with the other Dragon Masters who lived in the castle: Bo, Rori, Ana, and Petra.

"I told the others that Worm sent you a dream," Bo said when Drake came in.

"It was about a Rainbow Dragon," Drake explained. "Worm says she's in trouble. But that's all he knows."

Griffith nodded. "Very interesting," he said. "There is a legend about a Rainbow Dragon. She is the only one of her kind. She is very old, and very powerful. My guess is that this dragon must be sending messages to Worm somehow."

"Do you know where she lives?" Drake asked.

"I can't recall," Griffith said. "But I am sure we'll find information in one of our books. Let's get to the classroom!"

Drake wolfed down an apple, a hunk of cheese, and a piece of bread. Then the wizard and five Dragon Masters walked to the lowest level of the castle.

"What did the Rainbow Dragon look like in your dream?" Ana asked. Her dark eyes shone. "Was she beautiful?"

Drake nodded. "Yes. She had shimmering scales in rainbow colors."

"Big deal," said red-haired Rori. "What kinds of powers could a Rainbow Dragon have? Does she shoot color beams? She can't be as powerful as a Fire Dragon, like Vulcan."

"Maybe she has special powers," Petra said. "After all, Worm looks plain. But he is the most powerful dragon we know."

Rori frowned. Drake knew she couldn't argue with that. Worm could move or break things with the power of his mind. He could transport himself and others anywhere in the world in a flash.

They reached the classroom. Griffith started taking books off a shelf and handing them out.

The room was quiet as the Dragon Masters flipped through the pages.

Bo broke the silence. "I found something!" he cried. "Here is a story about a Rainbow Dragon that lives in the Kingdom of Ifri."

"Is that far from where we are, in the Kingdom of Bracken?" Petra asked.

"I know where Ifri is!" Ana said. She ran to a shelf. She came back and unrolled a map on the table.

"This is the Land of Pyramids, where I am from," she said. "And over here is the Kingdom of Ifri. It is a long way from my home, but my father has traveled there."

"What else does the story say?" Petra asked.

Bo read aloud, "The Rainbow Dragon has the powers of rain. Every year she comes out of her cave and brings rain to the land."

"Just like in my dream!" Drake said. "But then I saw her in her cave. She looked . . . trapped. And something was coming after her!"

"If the Rainbow Dragon is trapped, then she can't make rain," Rori said.

Ana gasped. "Oh no!" she cried. "Without rain, plants will die. There will be no food."

"I'm afraid you're right," Griffith agreed. "Ifri is in real trouble!"

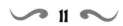

A NEW DRAGON MASTER?

W e've got to help the Rainbow Dragon!"
Drake said. "We need to go to Ifri!"

"Ifri is very big," Ana said, pointing at the
map. "How will we find the dragon?"

Drake shrugged. "Worm doesn't know
where she is. So he can't transport us to her
cave."

Petra looked at Griffith. "Can you use magic to find the Rainbow Dragon?"

Griffith stroked his long, white beard. "I can try."

Everyone followed the wizard to his workshop. He walked to a small table and took a cloth off a gazing ball. He bent over the glass globe and waved his hand over it.

The Dragon Masters watched the ball. A cloud of smoke swirled inside it.

Griffith frowned. "I cannot see anything," he said. "There is some kind of magic hiding the Rainbow Dragon."

Bo looked down at his Dragon Stone. "Does the Rainbow Dragon have a Dragon Master?" he asked.

"Excellent question, Bo!" Griffith said. "If we can find the Dragon Master, then maybe we can find the Rainbow Dragon."

He hurried over to a wooden box and opened it. Inside glittered a large, green stone — the Dragon Stone. Each Dragon Master's stone came from it.

"Dragon Stone, show me the Dragon Master of the Rainbow Dragon," Griffith asked.

Bright green light shot out of the stone. Moving pictures appeared inside the light.

A boy stood in front of a well. He pulled up a bucket and frowned. The well should have had water in it. But the bucket was empty. He showed it to a woman nearby.

"The well is dry," she told him. "It is like this all over Ifri."

Then the green light faded.

"Is that boy the Dragon Master?" Rori asked.

Griffith nodded. "Yes. He is the true Dragon Master chosen by the Dragon Stone," he said. "And this discovery brings us one step closer to finding the Rainbow Dragon."

The wizard clapped. "We must travel to Ifri and find this boy at once!"

A STRANGE MESSAGE

Worm can transport us to Ifri," Drake pointed out. "But how will we find the new Dragon Master once we land? The boy could be anywhere in Ifri."

"I have been working on a spell that can locate Dragon Masters," Griffith said. "I will get that ready. Drake and Ana, prepare your dragons for the journey. You two will come with me."

"Just Drake and Ana? What about the rest of us?" Rori asked.

"You must stay behind, to protect the castle," Griffith said.

Rori nodded. "Bo, Petra, and I will make sure nothing bad happens here while you're gone."

As she spoke, a sparkling blue bubble floated into Griffith's workshop.

"Look!" Petra cried.

POP! The bubble burst right in front of Griffith. A piece of paper fell into his hands. He opened it up.

"What does it say?" Ana asked.

"It is a message from the Wizard's Council," Griffith replied. Then his face went dark. "Drake, Ana, I am afraid I cannot go with you. I must deal with this message. But I trust that you will find the Rainbow Dragon. If you need help, transport back here right away."

Drake and Ana ran to the dragon caves and quickly returned to the Training Room with Worm and Kepri. Ana had put a saddle on Kepri's back.

They found Griffith looking down at the map of Ifri with Bo and Rori.

"One moment," Griffith said. "I'm putting the final spell on this map."

Griffith pointed at the map. Sparks flew from his finger.

"Map, help Drake and Ana roam. To the Dragon Master's home!" he rhymed.

The map glowed, and then it faded.

Griffith handed the map to Ana.

"This should show you the way once you land in Ifri," Griffith said. He opened a box and pulled out a Dragon Stone that dangled from a chain. He handed it to Drake. "Give this to the new Dragon Master when you see him."

Drake nodded. "Yes, Griffith." He tucked the stone into his pocket.

Petra ran up to them, out of breath.

"Wait!" she cried. She had a small bag in each hand. She gave one to Drake, and one to Ana. "I collected some food for your journey. And water."

"Thanks," Drake said, and Ana hugged Petra.

Then Ana touched Kepri with one hand, and Worm with the other. Drake touched Worm.

"Good luck!" Bo said.

"Hurry back!" Rori added.

Drake looked up at Worm. "Take us to the Land of Ifri!" he said.

Worm's body began to glow green. A bright, green light exploded in the Training Room.

Drake blinked. His body felt tingly. The green light faded, and he saw a blue sky and bright sun above his head.

"We're here!" Ana cheered.

Drake looked around. The land was very flat for as far as he could see. The tall grass was turning yellow. Some short trees popped up here and there, but their leaves were dying. There was no sign of a village.

"Which way should we go?" Drake asked.

Ana unrolled the map. A blue, glowing line appeared.

"Let's follow the magic map!" she said.

FOLLOW THE MAP

Ana and Drake walked across the grassy land. Kepri walked behind Ana, and Worm slithered behind Drake.

The hot sun shone overhead as they walked. Colorful birds flew from tree to tree.

"Most of the birds in Bracken are brown. Or gray," Drake said.

"Ifri is full of many creatures you won't find in Bracken," Ana told him.

"I hope we see more," Drake said. "But mostly, I want to find the Dragon Master!"

They walked and walked, following the map.

"My father said there are many beautiful waterfalls in Ifri," Ana remarked. "But we haven't seen any yet."

"*Everything* looks dried up," Drake said, looking at the yellow grass beneath his feet. "How much farther?"

"I don't know," she replied. "The map doesn't show where we're supposed to stop. The blue line just keeps getting longer as we walk."

Drake looked at the setting sun.

"It's getting late," he said.

"We can sleep under the stars," Ana said. "I've done it before, when I traveled with my father. Don't worry. I'll find us a good spot."

Ana soon found a spot inside a circle of trees. They both sat down in the grass.

"We'll camp here for the night," Ana said.

Drake nodded. "It feels good to rest." He opened the bag Petra had given him and took out a pouch filled with water. "And I'm so thirsty!"

He took a drink.

"Can I see the map?" Drake asked.

"Sure," Ana said. "There's just a blue dot on it now, since we've stopped."

Drake took the map from Ana. "There's got to be something here that shows us where the new Dragon Master's village is," he said. He took another sip of water — and the pouch slipped from his hand! Water spilled onto the map. The black ink faded. The blue dot disappeared.

"Drake!" Ana yelled. "What did you do?"

"It was an accident!" Drake yelled back.

"I know." Ana paused. "I'm sorry I yelled. But the spell is ruined."

Drake took a deep breath. He didn't want to fail Griffith. They had to rescue the Rainbow Dragon and save Ifri.

"Let's get some rest," he said. "We're both tired. Maybe the map will dry out overnight."

"I hope you're right," Ana said, yawning. "We'll check it in the morning."

The two Dragon Masters ate some apples and bread. The night air was chilly, so Worm curled his body around Drake. Ana snuggled against Kepri. They slept soundly.

When Drake opened his eyes, four enormous creatures surrounded their camp!

WILD FRIENDS

"Ana, wake up!" Drake yelled. "We're surrounded by dragons! Well — I *think* they're dragons!"

The four creatures were as big as dragons. But they had very long, skinny noses. They had gray, wrinkly skin instead of scales. Their big ears looked like wings to Drake.

Ana laughed. "They're not dragons, Drake," she said. "They're called elephants. And they're friendly. Well, usually they are."

Worm studied the elephants. Then his eyes began to glow. The elephants made trumpeting sounds with their trunks and shuffled their feet.

Drake's Dragon Stone glowed. He heard Worm's voice inside his head.

"Worm asked the elephants to help us. They know of a village not far from here," Drake told Ana. "They will lead us part of the way."

Ana looked down at the map. "That's a good thing, because the map still isn't working."

"Elephants to the rescue!" Drake said.

Drake and Ana ate breakfast. Then they followed the slow-moving elephants across the land. After a short time, they stopped at a shallow pool of water in the ground. The elephants sucked up the water in their long noses and then brought the water to their mouths. Worm and Kepri drank, too.

The elephants waved their trunks at Worm and walked away. Drake heard words inside his head.

The elephants told me how to get to the village. Follow me.

Drake motioned for Ana and Kepri to follow Worm.

"What about the Rainbow Dragon?" Drake asked Worm as they walked on. "Can you still feel her energy?"

It is weak, Worm replied. *Something keeps blocking my mind powers. I feel her, but her location is ... fuzzy.*

Just then, Ana cried, "Drake! Look! It's the village!"

Drake turned and saw a bunch of round houses with pointy tops. Lots of people were walking around.

Then Drake spotted the boy that the Dragon Stone had shown them.

"There he is!" Drake yelled. "It's the new Dragon Master!"

THE CHOSEN ONE

Drake and Ana ran over to the new Dragon Master. The boy looked up at Worm and Kepri. His eyes got wide.

All the villagers began staring at the dragons. No one ran or started screaming. They actually moved closer.

"Are those . . . dragons?" the boy asked. "We have many legends about dragons here. But we have never seen any."

Drake nodded. "Yes, they are dragons," he said. "I'm Drake, and this is my dragon, Worm."

"And I'm Ana. My dragon's name is Kepri," Ana said with a smile.

"I am Obi," the boy said. "Welcome to our village. What brings you here?"

"We came to find *you*," Drake said. "You need to help the Rainbow Dragon."

Obi's mouth dropped open. The villagers all began to talk at once. A man and a woman walked up behind Obi.

"We are Obi's parents," the man said. "Please tell us where you are from, and what you know about the Rainbow Dragon."

"We came from the Kingdom of Bracken in the north," Ana replied.

Drake patted Worm's neck. "My dragon got a message from the Rainbow Dragon. She told Worm that she is in trouble."

Obi's parents looked at each other.

"This is what we have feared," Obi's father said. "The rains have not come. Water is hard to find. Plants are dying. We will soon run out of food."

"But how can Obi help?" Obi's mother asked.

"Our wizard has a Dragon Stone," Drake said. "It showed us that Obi has a special connection with the Rainbow Dragon. He is her Dragon Master. He may be the only one who can help her."

Obi shook his head. "That makes no sense," he said. "The Rainbow Dragon does not need a master. She is very powerful."

"Even the most powerful dragons need help sometimes," Ana said. "Do you know where she might be?"

Obi shook his head. "The legend says she lives in a cave somewhere," he replied. "She has never been seen. But when the rains come and a rainbow appears, we know that she has helped us."

Drake took the piece of the Dragon Stone from his pocket. "You are her Dragon Master. You can use your connection with her to help us find her."

Obi's father spoke up. "It is our good fortune that these visitors came here. You must help them, Obi."

"How can *I* help?" Obi asked. "I am just a boy. Someone else should go. A warrior. Or a healer. Or a teacher."

Ana took the Dragon Stone from Drake and put it around Obi's neck.

"The Dragon Stone picked you," she said. "You are the chosen one."

Obi looked at his parents. He looked down at the stone. Then he took a deep breath.

"All right," he said. "I will help you!"

"Yes!" Ana cheered.

"But I do not know how to find the Rainbow Dragon," Obi said.

"Worm is getting some fuzzy energy signals from the Rainbow Dragon," Drake explained. "He can lead us in the right direction."

"Then your link with the Rainbow Dragon will take us the rest of the way," Ana said. "Your Dragon Stone will glow green when you connect with her. She will lead you to her."

Obi's mother kissed her son on the head. "Be safe. The village is counting on you."

The villagers waved as Obi left with Drake, Ana, and the dragons.

THE JOURNEY

The Dragon Masters and the dragons made their way across the grassland.

"What is your kingdom like?" Obi asked as they walked.

"Well, Bracken is not flat like here," Drake replied. "There are mountains."

"And there are a lot more trees," Ana added.

"I used to live on a farm," Drake told Obi. "One year, we had a summer with very little rain. A lot of the crops died. It was scary."

Obi nodded. "Without our crops, there will be no food to eat."

Drake picked up his water pouch and frowned. "Rats. I'm almost out of water."

"Me, too," Ana added.

"I think there is a watering hole around here," Obi said. He walked ahead of Ana and Drake, looking at the ground. Then he broke away from the path.

"Where are you going?" Drake asked. He and Ana hurried to catch up to Obi.

"These are animal tracks," Obi explained, pointing to the ground. "And they lead right . . . here."

He pushed through some bushes, and they stepped into a clearing. A small pool of water bubbled up from the dirt.

"Wow!" Drake cried.

"You found water!" Ana said happily.

They filled their pouches with water. Worm took a drink, too.

Then Obi led them back through the bushes.

Suddenly, Obi froze. He stopped Drake with his arm.

A strange animal stood in the grass ahead of them. It looked like a very big, very hairy pig with long, white tusks!

The animal's ears twitched. Then it turned around and locked eyes with Drake.

CHAPTER 9

KWAKU!

bi put a finger to his lips. "*Shh!* Don't move," he whispered to Drake and Ana. "It's a warthog! If you make any fast movements, it might attack."

Obi raised his arms above his head and crept up to the warthog. Then he made a very loud, scary noise.

ROOOAAAAAR!

Frightened, the warthog squealed and scrambled away.

"Wow, Obi! That was awesome!" Drake said. "You sounded like a big, scary cat."

"I was pretending to be a lion," Obi said. "Do you have lions in Bracken?"

Drake shook his head.

"They are big, fierce cats," Obi explained.

Ana smiled at Obi. "You are very smart and brave. I think you were born to be a Dragon Master."

"Yes," Drake agreed. "You found water for us. You scared away the warty hog. You're amazing!"

Obi gave them both a shy smile. They caught up to Worm and Kepri, who had started moving again.

A few minutes later, Obi's Dragon Stone began to glow faintly.

"Obi, look!" Drake cried, pointing. "Your stone is glowing. The Rainbow Dragon is trying to connect with you."

Worm stopped.

Obi must lead us the rest of the way, he told Drake. *His connection is stronger than mine.*

"Worm says you should lead us," Drake told Obi.

"How do I do that?" Obi asked.

"Can you feel the pull of your dragon's energy?" Ana said.

Obi closed his eyes. "It's weak, but I can feel it!" he said, his voice rising with excitement. "It's like . . . she's in my head."

"Great! Now walk toward that energy," Ana instructed.

Obi started walking. They followed him to a low hill. A big hole in the hill led to an underground tunnel.

Obi gazed into the tunnel. "I . . . I think she is in here," he said.

Ana looked up at Kepri. "Can you please light the way for us?"

A white ball of light floated out of Kepri's mouth. It hung in the air, lighting up the dark tunnel.

The ball floated down the tunnel, and the others followed it.

They went a short way and then stopped.
A thick spiderweb blocked the entrance to a
cave!

"Whoa! A *very* big spider must have made
this," Drake said.

Obi gasped. "Kwaku!" he cried.

"What's a kwaku?" Drake asked.

"Kwaku is a giant spider that my people tell stories about," Obi explained. "Sometimes he is a hero. Sometimes he makes trouble."

"Are they true stories?" Drake asked.

"I thought they were just legends," Obi said. "But look at this web! Only Kwaku could have spun it."

Suddenly, Drake's Dragon Stone began to glow. He heard Worm's voice inside his head.

Obi is right. Kwaku has trapped the Rainbow Dragon inside her cave!

STUCK IN A WEB

rake ran to the giant web blocking the entrance to the cave. He started pulling on the strands.

"I can't break the web!" he said. "It is too strong and sticky!"

"Drake, stop!" Ana said. "If there is a giant spider behind there, we need a plan."

She turned to Obi. "In the stories about Kwaku, how is he defeated?" she asked.

"I don't think he has ever been beaten. Kwaku is a magical trickster. He usually uses tricks to escape," Obi said.

"There must be a way to stop him," Drake said.

"Well, some stories say he works for the ruler of the sun. So maybe the sun can stop Kwaku?" Obi guessed.

"Hmm," Ana said. "Kepri might not be the ruler of the sun. But she has the powers of the sun! Maybe she can break through the web and fight Kwaku's magic."

Ana turned to Kepri. "Use a sunbeam on the web!"

Kepri opened her mouth and shot a strong beam of sunlight at the thick spiderweb. The strands of the web began to shimmer. Then they disappeared!

"It worked!" Drake cried.

Obi put a finger to his lips. "Quiet."

They stepped into the cave. The ball of white sunlight still floated in the air, lighting the dark space.

Drake and Ana gasped.

A dragon with a very long body was wrapped in a cocoon of spider silk. Through the silk, Drake could see the dragon's rainbow-colored scales.

"The Rainbow Dragon!" Obi cried.

"Kepri, use another sunbeam to get rid of the cocoon!" Ana commanded.

The Sun Dragon aimed a strong beam of sunlight at the Rainbow Dragon. The webs began to shimmer, but before they could disappear...

Click, click, click! A loud, clicking sound began to echo through the cave. Kepri stopped shooting her sunbeam and turned toward the sound.

A giant spider crawled out of the shadows! His eight long legs were black with yellow stripes. His round body had a black-and-yellow pattern. Eight round, black eyes stared at the Dragon Masters and their dragons. Drake, Ana, and Obi started to slowly back up.

Eeeeeeeee! With a cry, the spider scurried toward them. Kepri and Worm charged forward, protecting the Dragon Masters.

"Kepri, hit him with sunlight!" Ana yelled.

Kepri aimed a beam of sunlight at Kwaku. The spider jumped up to avoid it. He hung upside down from the ceiling of the cave.

In a flash, he shot webs at Kepri.

The webs wrapped around her mouth. Kepri couldn't fight back. The webs magically grew and twisted all around Kepri's body.

"Kepri!" Ana cried.

Worm's body began to glow green. But before he could use his powers, Kwaku hit him with webs, too. The webs wrapped around Worm. Within seconds, he was trapped inside a cocoon.

"Quick, hide!" Drake yelled to Ana and Obi. "We can't help the dragons if Kwaku gets us, too!"

The friends raced behind a big rock. Drake touched his Dragon Stone.

"Worm, can you hear me?" he whispered.

Drake's Dragon Stone glowed faintly. Drake heard a muffled voice in his head.

He turned to Ana and Obi. "Worm is trying to tell me something, but I can't understand him," he said. "The cocoon must be blocking Worm's powers!"

"I can't hear Kepri's voice in my head, either," Ana whispered.

"What now?" Drake asked. "We can't fight Kwaku without our dragons!"

A STRONG CONNECTION

rake, Ana, and Obi stayed hidden behind the rock. But the clicking sound of the giant spider grew louder as he got closer.

Click, click, click.

"We should go get help," Obi whispered.

"Who will help us?" Drake asked.

Click, click, click.

"We can't stay here," Ana said. "Kwaku is going to trap us in cocoons, too!"

Obi stood up. His Dragon Stone was glowing.

"Obi, get down!" Drake hissed.

Obi didn't listen to Drake. He stared at the Rainbow Dragon.

Kwaku spotted Obi with one of his eight eyes.

"Watch out, Obi! Kwaku will hit you with one of his webs!" Drake yelled.

Obi didn't run. He talked to the Rainbow Dragon.

"Our village needs you," he said. "Please help us."

Then Obi's Dragon Stone began to glow brighter . . . and brighter . . . and brighter!

"Whoa!" Drake told Ana. "I've never seen a Dragon Stone glow like that before. It's even brighter than Worm when he uses his powers!"

The bright green light filled the cave. The Dragon Masters had to shield their eyes.

Eeeeeeeeeeeeeeee! Kwaku shrieked.

As the powerful light grew, he skittered deep into the cave.

The light faded. Drake looked around. The cocoons around the dragons were shimmering, just like when Kepri's sunlight hit the giant web.

The cocoons disappeared. Drake and Ana ran to their dragons.

Ana patted Kepri's head.

"Worm! Are you okay?" Drake asked.

I am fine, Worm replied.

Drake smiled and glanced over at Obi.

The new Dragon Master was standing next to the Rainbow Dragon. She was free of the cocoon, and hovering above the floor.

"She's so beautiful," Ana whispered.

The Rainbow Dragon's colorful scales shimmered in the dim light of the cave. She had a long, snakelike body like Worm's. She did not have wings.

Obi turned to Drake and Ana. "She says it's time to make it rain. And she wants me to go with her."

Drake nodded.

Obi climbed onto the Rainbow Dragon's back. Then they floated out of the cave, past Drake, Ana, and their dragons.

Ana nudged Drake. "Let's go!"

They ran outside, followed by Worm and Kepri. The sun shone brightly in the blue sky.

The Rainbow Dragon flew up, up above the grassy lands, with Obi on her back.

"I'll meet you back at the village!" Obi called down.

Obi and the dragon flew higher and higher.
Gray clouds appeared in the sky.

Then Drake felt one cold, wet drop on his
cheek.

"Rain!" he cheered.

DRAGONS IN THE SKY

More clouds filled the sky. The rain began to fall harder.

"Obi will be busy for a while," Drake said. "Let's go tell his parents what happened."

Ana nodded. She touched Kepri with one hand and Worm with the other.

Worm transported them to the village in a flash of green light. They found the villagers standing outside in the rain.

Obi's parents ran up to them.

"Where is Obi?" Obi's mother asked.

"He is safe!" Drake replied. "Kwaku the spider was keeping the Rainbow Dragon prisoner. Obi freed her. They are both up in the sky now, making rain."

Obi's mother took Ana by the hand. "Come, both of you. I think this will be a long rain. Step inside our hut, where it is warm and dry."

Obi's mother fed them bowls of hot stew.

Just as they were finishing, a shout came from outside the hut.

"Look!"

Drake, Ana, and Obi's parents rushed outside.

The clouds were floating away. The sun was shining. The sky was bright blue. And the Rainbow Dragon was floating in the sky. Her body curved, just like a rainbow. Her colorful scales shimmered brightly. Obi sat on her back, beaming happily.

Everyone stared at the sight, amazed.

Then Ana's Dragon Stone began to glow. She smiled.

"Kepri wants to fly, too," she said.

Ana climbed onto Kepri's back. Kepri flew up into the sky. Misty waterdrops filled the air. She shot a beam of sunlight from her mouth. The light hit the water droplets and made a rainbow right underneath the Rainbow Dragon.

Drake grinned. "It's a double rainbow!"

DAYO'S STORY

Kepri and the Rainbow Dragon flew down from the sky. Obi slid off the Rainbow Dragon's back and ran to his parents.

"Mom! Dad!" he cried.

"Hooray for Obi!" the villagers cheered.

Obi's Dragon Stone began to glow.

"The Rainbow Dragon wants me to tell you her story," he said. "Her name is Dayo."

"Dayo," Ana repeated, hopping off Kepri. "That's a cool name!"

"Did she say how Kwaku trapped her in her cave?" Drake asked.

"Kwaku tricked her," Obi went on. "He told the Rainbow Dragon he knew the most beautiful song in the world. She asked to hear it. But the song was really a spell that made her fall asleep. Then he spun a cocoon around her."

Some of the villagers gasped.

"Why would he do that?" Ana asked.

"Kwaku was mad at Dayo," Obi explained. "The last time the rains came, water flooded his den. He trapped Dayo because he didn't want that to happen ever again."

Obi's father nodded. "He is a tricky one!" he said.

"Dayo couldn't move, but her mind was still powerful," Obi continued. "She called out for help. And Drake's dragon, Worm, heard her."

Drake patted Worm. "And then Worm told me," he said. "And then we found Obi."

"Dayo is grateful to you both, and your dragons," Obi told Drake and Ana.

Two young boys ran into the village.

"The waterfall is flowing again!" one of them shouted.

The villagers cheered and hugged one another.

"I'm glad the Rainbow Dragon is safe now," Ana said. "But what if Kwaku tries to trick her again?"

"Dayo says she knows not to trust Kwaku ever again," Obi replied. "And now that she and I have connected, she will call on me if she is in trouble."

Obi looked down at his glowing Dragon Stone. A sad look crossed his face.

"Dayo says that she must go back to her cave," he said. "She must watch over the land, like she always has."

He hugged his dragon. "I will miss you, Dayo," he said.

The Rainbow Dragon wrapped her body around Obi, giving him a quick hug.

Then she floated up into the sky and flew away.

"I was hoping that you and Dayo could come back to Bracken and train with us," Drake said.

"We cannot, but thank you," Obi said. "The Rainbow Dragon belongs in this land. And so do I."

"I understand," Drake replied.

Obi's father stepped forward. "Thank you for helping our village," he said. "You will always be welcome here."

"Thank you," Drake said. "Now we must get home. Our friends will be getting worried about us."

"Good-bye!" Ana called out.

Drake and Ana touched their dragons. Then Worm transported the four of them back to Bracken in a flash of green light.

TROUBLE AT THE CASTLE

"Diego, what are you doing?!"

The first thing Drake and Ana heard when they landed in the Training Room was Griffith's voice. He sounded angry. They quickly left Worm and Kepri and followed the sound to the classroom.

"Please stop!" Griffith was yelling at a short, round wizard. Diego was Griffith's friend, and he had helped the Dragon Masters many times. But now he was making a mess of the classroom. He took book after book off the shelf and tossed each one on the floor.

"Where is it? It has got to be here!" Diego muttered to himself. He ignored Griffith.

"Diego, calm down!" Griffith ordered.

Suddenly Diego held up a book. "I found it!" he cried. He spun around, facing Griffith.

Griffith gasped. His mouth dropped open in surprise.

That's when Drake noticed something — Diego's eyes were red!

"Diego! Let us help you!" Drake cried, but Diego had a special talent. He could transport, just like Worm.

Poof! The wizard disappeared.

Rori, Bo, and Petra came running into the classroom.

"What's all the yelling about?" Rori asked. Then she stopped. "Drake! Ana! You're back!"

"Yes, and we saved the Rainbow Dragon," Ana said. "But that's not why Griffith was yelling. Diego was just here!"

"His eyes were red — the color of Maldred's dark magic," Drake said. "I think he was under a spell!"

Everyone was quiet. Maldred was an evil wizard. He had attacked King Roland's castle and tried to take the dragons away. The Dragon Masters, Griffith, and Diego had stopped him.

Bo turned to Griffith. "But you and Diego sent Maldred to the Wizard's Council Prison," he said. "He can't use magic while he's in there."

"That is what the council warned me about earlier . . ." the wizard replied. "Maldred has escaped."

"No!" Rori yelled. She balled her hands into fists. "We need to find him!"

"What would he want with Diego?" Petra asked.

"It looks like Maldred has used Diego to steal a book from me," Griffith said as he riffled through the bookshelf. "But — no, wait, it couldn't be . . ." His face turned pale. "Diego took my book about the Naga, a dragon of legend."

"Is that bad?" Drake asked.

Griffith nodded. "Very bad. If Maldred is seeking the Naga, then the whole world is in danger!"

TRACEY WEST was once lucky enough to see a double rainbow, and she hopes you'll get to see one, too.

Tracey has written dozens of books for kids. She writes in the house she shares with her husband, her three stepkids (when they're home from college), and her animal friends. She has three dogs and one cat, who sits on her desk when she writes! Thankfully, the cat does not weigh as much as a dragon.

DAMIEN JONES lives with his wife and son in Cornwall — the home of the legend of King Arthur. Cornwall even has its very own castle! On clear days you can see for miles from the top of the castle, making it the perfect lookout for dragons.

Damien has illustrated children's books. He has also animated films and television programs. He works in a studio surrounded by figures of mystical characters that keep an eye on him as he draws.

DRAGON MASTERS
WAKING THE RAINBOW DRAGON

Questions and Activities

Drake has a dream at the beginning of the story. Who sends him the dream? Why?

Why is the Rainbow Dragon important to the Kingdom of Ifri? Turn back to pages 11 and 36.

How did Kwaku trick the Rainbow Dragon? (Hint! Look back on page 79.)

At the end of the story, the Dragon Masters discover that Diego is under Maldred's spell. What do you think the dark wizard wants with Diego? Predict what will happen in the next book. Write your own beginning chapter, and draw your own action-packed pictures.

Drake and Ana see elephants and a warthog in the Kingdom of Ifri. What wild animal would you most like to see in real life? Where does this animal live? Using nonfiction books and the Internet, learn more about this animal.

The Fireside Watergate

The Fireside Watergate

by Nicholas von Hoffman and Garry Trudeau

Sheed & Ward: New York

To Susy P. Dooley and
R. "Ron" Ziegler, III, Jr.

"What really hurts in matters of this sort is not the fact that they occur, because overzealous people in campaigns do things that are wrong. What really hurts is if you try to cover it up."

Himself, San Clemente,
August 29, 1972

Contents

"It's incredible, Gordo! Over $50,000 worth of equipment, including tape recorders, transmitters, antennas and walkie-talkies! Now this is what I call a first-rate burglary attempt!"

1. The Last Encampment of the Grand Army of the Bay of Pigs

America was embarking on a new political experience. The fix was in, the cabinet was dissolved and Congress had been told to go stuff it. The country was going to be run by an Emergency Counter-Intelligence Coalition government. Locked in the Oval Room, working out his problem in silence, was the boss. The Defrocked Quaker was attended by his two Christian Scientist lay readers who issued their orders to a cabala of Cuban real estate operators through intermediary layers of ex-third echelon advertising executives, young right wing lawyers with shit-eating grins, superannuated spies, bagmen, goons, looters, alcoholics, inefficiency experts and fanatics of all ages.

The Cubans are the key, though. Cubans are obedient, trustworthy and the highly satisfactory kind of democrats who will fight for liberty but not use it. Manolo, the valet who lays out his blue business suit before he takes his lonely walks on the beach, is a Cuban. Manolo who feeds him his cottage cheese with catsup. Bebe Rebozo who takes him for boat rides and holds his hand during his enumerated crises is a Cuban.

So when Daniel Ellsberg stole the Pentagon Papers they told the cheese eater they'd get some Cubans on the case.

13

There was no case, though. Ellsberg and his pal had confessed on television that they'd done it so that there was nothing more to do than to try 'em, put 'em in jail and forget 'em. But the great recluse couldn't believe the simple truth because he doesn't believe the truth is simple. There had to be a plot because if he'd stolen the Pentagon Papers it would have been part of a big plot.

We ride again, amigo mio. Bernard Barker, ex-Havana cop for Fulgencio Batista, ex-CIA Bay of Pigger, Cuban and Miami realtor, comes home to dinner and finds a note stuck on his door saying, "If you are the same Bernard Barker I once knew, come on over and have a drink at the Trade Winds. Eduardo." Unable to buy tickets to "No, No, Nanette," but smitten with nostalgia, Bernardo drives over to Miami Beach to have a drink with his old CIA commandante, Eduardo, alias Edward L. Warren, alias Edward J. Hamilton, alias E. Howard Hunt, Jr.

Between drinks, embrazos and reminiscences, E. Howard Eduardo sticks an index finger into Bernardo's gut and tells him he's getting old and fat. No, I still got the cojones for freedom fighting, replies Bernardo, and they order another round of Cuba libres. A night of rum, patriotism and the scent of money. The Miami realtor laps it up and the two middle-age fuck-ups sit there telling each other that history is calling them.

It was. Ordinarily history rations its great disasters one to a customer. One Spanish Armada for Phillip II, one Waterloo for Napoleon, but for you, Bernardo, and for you, E. Howard Eduardo, there is the Bay of Pigs *and* Watergate. Salud!

At the time, Bernardo's ancient commandante, with whom he once sloshed through the rain forests of Honduras prepping for the Bay of Pigs, was a 52-year-old ex-spook, a character out of his own fantasies who wrote adventure stories and then gave his real life agents aliases from the

names of the people in his books. E. Howard Hunt, Jr.'s books have titles like "I Came To Kill" and "Murder On The Rocks." They contain passages like, "Mind blowing hot pants concealed her delta as she flexed the knee of one long and lovely leg . . . stretching back her arms, she resembled Athena in full flight. And just as braless. I gobbled some of my drink." If there had been one literary critic, or one literate in the White House, we wouldn't have had a Watergate. But you can also say that if the Democratic National Committee had had offices at 1168 19th Street we wouldn't have had a Watergate. The 1168 19th Street Scandal is not a name that would catch on.

Everything had to break right up and down the whole chain of command. There had to be plenty of cottage cheese, a suitably named place called Watergate and an E. Howard Eduardo who wouldn't wake up the next morning with a rum hangover and groan about the silly things he and Bernardo had said the night before. E. Howard didn't, for this was his biggest chance to go ape and act it all out. During those 20 years at the CIA he'd been forced to work under a few restraints, but now in his retirement he could be a $100 a day "consultant" at the White House where he had an office, a desk full of incriminating papers and a pistol.

The Mafia calls it a job, while the White House calls it a mission and this mission was to break into the office of Daniel Ellsberg's shrink and get the documents. What documents? Does a man who's the central figure of a conspiracy pay $50 an hour three times a week so he can tell his shrink who will write it down so a band of freedom-crazed Cubans will break in and steal it? You forget the cheese eating recluse had gone to a shrink. So it follows he must have told *his* head shrinker about *his* conspiracy, and for therapy the doctor had prescribed running for president, and if you get elected that proves you're not crazy, everybody else is.

The call from Washington to Miami came. The mission is

go. No aborting this time, amigo mio. Get two top men and meet me at the Beverly Wilshire Hotel. I'll run over to Virginia and get a mess of wigs, beards and phony ID's from the CIA and meet you in Los Angeles. Bernardo does what he's told, picks his two top salesmen and they rendezvous at the headshrinker's office where they pose for souvenir pictures outside and then break in, open the files, search the records and find nothing but Ellsberg's address and telephone number, which you can get by dialing 411.

Later, when this burglary came out in the papers, it was reported that they'd failed to find whatever they were looking for. It's never been brought out but they were after Ellsberg's phone number; they didn't want to call information. The operator might have recognized the voice, and besides, such a call would have violated the rule that all missions were to be run with the maximum possible risk and the minimal possible reward. Nothing was to be done simply if a complicated method could be invented. All spy missions were to be featherbedded. Don't use one spook if there's room in the car for five. This doesn't make any sense if you're in the delicatessen business, but the Washington intelligence community calls it safeguard redundancy or a marginal repetitive random protective reaction configuration.

It works. The recluse got the phone number, called up Ellsberg and told him, "Look, I know you stole the cottage cheese, and I want it back." Ellsberg kept demanding to know, "How did you get my phone number?" Better he should have asked the LAPD safe and loft squad. They'd found an important dangling clue, a brochure advertising choice Florida vacation and retirement properties, but since the detectives investigating the case already had some nice beach frontage down near San Diego, there was no need to follow up.

Having done so well, the commandante decided to give Bernardo a bonus sales opportunity. Ellsberg and William

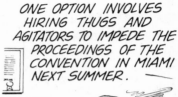

Kunstler were going to be in Washington talking on the Capitol steps. As Bernardo explained later, "These people would probably desecrate the tomb of Mr. Hoover. It was also said to me that these people would wave a Viet Cong flag." The answer to this threat was another call from E. Howard Eduardo, Jr. Hunt to assemble a squad of 10 elite Hispano-Miami realtors to fly to Washington, infiltrate the crowd on the Capitol steps and beat the shit out of anyone refusing to buy a $40,000 split level bungalow.

Several days later the White House announced the economy was firming, housing starts were up, but there would now be still more important work for these economic stimulators. First the group would be enlarged to include some non-Cubans, G. Gordon Liddy, alias George F. Leonard, alias George Russell, and James W. McCord, Jr. alias Edward J. Warren, alias Edward J. Martin and Alfred C. Baldwin, III, alias Bill Johnson.

There is much about this phase that isn't yet known. For example, why wasn't James W. McCord, Jr. known as J. William McCord, Jr? Another question that Watergate investigators haven't answered is why there were so many Jr's and so many III's but no II's. This should have alerted the conspirators that something was missing in their plans, but even more serious was the name problem. In spook work of this kind, you never use your real name with other members of the team, but only with the public at large or when charging something on your credit card.

Even so, the system might have worked if only McCord had a good memory for names, but he was new on his job as chief security officer for the Committee to Re-Elect the President (CREEP). He hadn't had much practice at that sort of thing since his last job was to walk around the CIA parking lot in Virginia with a police dog and catch girl and boy spies making out in the back seats.

Thus at the key meeting between Alfred C. Baldwin III, G. Gordon Liddy, Jr. and E. Howard Hunt, Jr., a/k/a

Eduardo, things hadn't gone well. "I want you guys to meet Al," McCord said, but he got a nudge in the ribs as Al whispered, "I thought my name was Bill."

"It is Bill," McCord replied. "Did I say Al? I made a mistake there. This isn't Al, fellas, this is Bill . . . Bill, I wancha to meet George F. Leonard."

"Hi, George," said Al who was really Bill, but nobody said hi back to him. Silence in the room until McCord asked, "Is George F. Leonard with us today?" "No," a voice answered, "George F. Leonard isn't here on Thursdays and Mondays. On those days George Russell takes his place and this is Monday."

"Say, Ed," said Al who is Bill to McCord who may have been Edward J. Martin or Edward J. Hamilton, "wouldn't ·it help to write it down . . . in code so nobody'd know?"

"What's going on around here?" asked Eduardo. "McCord's not Ed. I'm Edward J. Hamilton." An angry discussion then ensued as to who had dibs on being Edward J. and while they were shouting at each other, McCord admitted the name book had been lost or stolen. The word "stolen" had no sooner been spoken than all the agents in the room realized the McGoverns may have swiped it.

As a stop gap measure it was decided that Al who is Bill would be called Base Unit, and Edward J. who is really El Commandante Eduardo would be Able Fox, while Edward J. Martin who is really James W. McCord, Jr. but should be J. William McCord Jr. would be Unable Fox. Nobody could remember what they'd agreed about G. Gordon Liddy, so they decided to call him Gordon and call everybody else The Cubans.

They realized they had to work fast. There was a cottage cheese shortage, the McGoverns might have the book with their real names in it and CREEP headquarters was screaming for action. The Big Boys had already put out a quarter of a million dollars for information that would prove a connection between George McGovern and Larry

O'Brien, the Chairman of the Democratic National Committee. If it could be shown that McGovern and O'Brien knew each other, that would make many people believe that McGovern was a Democrat with a resulting massive defection from that party at the polls on election day.

So far all that the team had been able to come up with was a recording of tapped telephone conversations of the ex-hippie who ran the mimeograph machine in the DNC talking about the night he'd gotten two female Scoop Jackson volunteers in bed with him. G. Gordon Liddy had slipped the transcription into special envelopes, called Gemstone envelopes, that were reserved for exciting but socially unredeeming matter and rushed it over to the Big Boys.

"Hell, that's no good, there're no pictures," the Boys had said, "You better get on the stick," they told Liddy, who was feeling desperate and under the gun now. He'd been the one who'd come over to the meeting with the Big Boys and showed them with flow charts and visual aids how they were going to rent a yacht in Miami, stock it with hookers, cameras and tape recorders and then lure McGovern and O'Brien on board. He'd promised the pictures would show linkage between the two, but they'd used separate staterooms so when the pictures came back from the drugstore all they'd shown is O'Brien likes redheads.

"What the hell good is that," the biggest of the Big Boys had shouted at Liddy. "Well, she's a red head, a *red* head, a RED head, if you get what I mean. Isn't that good for something," Liddy had pleaded, but the Biggest Boy had crushed him by reminding him of the color of Pat's hair — "We can't use it. Get me something good," he'd told Liddy.

"I know where I can get ya some quick, dirty Muskie . . . in Hank Greenspun's safe in the offices of the Las Vegas Sun."

"Well, get it, you dumb bastard," said the Biggest of the Boys impolitely as he bit the stem of his pipe in two. Dirty

Muskie was not the most valuable commodity around but the Biggest of the Boys was himself under pressure to come up with some fast cottage cheese.

Time again for Los Cubanos de los Real Estatos. The plan was a relatively simple one, not the kind of thing G. Gordon Liddy liked, but time was short. Everybody would fly out to the Beverly Wilshire which would be used, as they say in the CIA, as a "safe house," meaning a place you can take a girl and not have to worry about cameras. Since the maid service in that hotel is particularly good there are a lot of "sterile phones" in the building which is important if you're in counter-intelligence, prone to catch cold, as happens when you're out in the cold and can't come in from it, and you forgot your vitamin C.

After everybody had arrived they would meet in Eduardo's room, number 16, where, to use the parlance of the trade again, "buck slips" would be passed on a need-to-know basis and the entire group subsequently labeled The Plumbers (even though George Meany has repeatedly said they don't have a card in his union), the whole group would be given a "read out" on the prospective "bag job" on the Greenspun safe.

So far so good. El Commandante got up, gave everyone their buck slips, their money and a freedom medal. Then he explained there had been a slight hitch. He'd left his red wig and two microphones hidden in simulated Chap-stick tubes, plus an ITT tout sheet on the next Kentucky Derby in Dita Beard's Denver hospital room. Also, did anybody happen to have a little .25 caliber ammunition for his Colt automatic which he'd absent-mindedly forgotten to leave in his White House office?

Then for the first time they were all told that the object was all the dirty Muskie they could carry out of Hank Greenspun's safe. The escape plan was easy enough. Two automobiles equipped with the latest anti-pollution catalytic converters and driven by two croupiers from Ceasar's

22

"Hi, folks. Won't you join me in voting for my friend Ed Muskie?"

Palace, so nobody would suspect, would whisk them to a private airport where Howard Hughes and Clifford Irving would personally pilot them in two World War II all-plywood planes to Costa Rica where they would participate in a classified real estate seminar. The plywood was to help them escape radar detection and thereby avoid being confused with the marijuana smugglers who clog up the airlanes around Las Vegas. At the same time, all the dirty Muskie would be sealed in Gemstone envelopes and sent special delivery to Washington where, God willing and the Post Office cooperating, the Big Boys would have it in a matter of days, or at least weeks.

The bag job was successful, but for a second time the contents of the loot was disappointing. They came away with no dirty Muskie, but a lot of dirty Nixon, namely the originals of the famous "Canuck" letter written by a double agent from The Washington Post and the master copy of the forgery of the Muskie Florida primary campaign letter accusing Hubert Humphrey of luring hot-assed pieces of jail bait into his motel room with farm subsidies and then plunkin' them.

It had been this letter which cost Humphrey the election. The legendary Minnesotan might have saved himself if he'd denied the accusations, but vanity got to him, and his headquarters issued a statement saying the charges proved that in the last days of the Johnson administration he had not been forced to undergo a most humiliating amputation. This was too much even for Humphrey's most loyal followers. At a West Palm Beach Haddassah meeting, they'd shouted things at him like "Show us! 'Humbert Humbert' you're not!" Faced with a choice of getting a medical certificate from Lyndon Johnson, the Pedernales pecker popper, or unzipping on state-wide TV, old HHH had withdrawn from the race.

It didn't work out any too good for Muskie either. People all over Florida were asking each other if they wanted a

24

man controlling the pushbutton of destiny who was opti-
mistic enough to think Hubert had anything left to get up
and salute the flag with.

The Big Boys still weren't satisfied. "For chrissakes,
Liddy, did you call that dirty Muskie? That job cost a lot of
money, first class round trip tickets to Las Vegas for you and
coach for that gang of spick cemetery lot salesmen, and you
come back with the original Muskie forgery. You're so
dumb you couldn't find a hooker in Miami. We know we
forged the letter," the Biggest of the Big Boys said rudely as
he spat out pieces of his pipe. Then his eyes slitted up, and
wow! was he ugly! His eyeballs looked like the barrels of
the machine guns in the slots of a Brinks armored truck and
all over his chin was spit and pieces of black plastic from his
pipe stem. "I didn't pay a quarter of a million dollars to
have you keep going out and getting incriminating evidence
on *us*. I have my deniability to worry about and you're ruin-
ing it with that crap. You get over to that damn Watergate
and you find the little book with the names in it that
Eduardo lost so we can end the confusion in the CREEP
payroll department. We have to know the names of the
people working for us. I don't know if I'm paying some of
you three times and some of you nothing. And you get the
goods on McGovern. You can't tell me that man's a prairie
radical. I know he's a Democrat and I want the proof," the
Chairman of the Big Boys said impolitely.

"Mr. Big Boy . . . " Liddy began.

"Look me in the eyes, and stop looking like one of your
greasers trying to sell Martha a condominium."

"I can't look you in the eyes, Mr. Big Boy," said a trem-
bling G. Gordon Liddy. "Then gimme another pipe stem
and get the hell out of here," Big Boy replied loudly as he
expectorated the crumbs of the last one into an empty cottage cheese container.

Liddy backed out the door promising to preserve the
Biggest of the Big Boy's deniability and swearing that he'd

25

get the right kind of incriminating evidence even if he had to order Eduardo to forge it. Back at his desk his faithful secretary, Sally Harmony, fed the shaken Liddy a tuna fish on white sandwich with the crusts cut off and waxed his moustache. Thus refreshed and composed, he called a meeting of The Plumbers for nine o'clock the next morning, but at eight thirty before all of the real estate salesmen had assembled another telegram from George Meany arrived: "PAY DUES OR DON'T USE NAME STOP PICKET LINE HELD UP BY MORNING TRAFFIC BUT ON ITS WAY SIGNED BOSS UNION PLUMBER."

Although some months later when she testified before the Ervin Senate Committee investigating Watergate, she couldn't remember the incident, the truth is that Liddy, on receipt of the Meany telegram, immediately sent Sally Harmony out for another tuna fish sandwich — that was her cover — and told her to stop off at the AFL-CIO and pay the Cubans' dues. "And bring back a receipt," he called after her, explaining, *If we get caught we're going to need a lot of evidence to shred." A half hour later she was back with the covering sandwich and a receipt from Meany with a note saying, "Ok, but what about the initiation fee?"*

Now all was in readiness for the climactic effort to save Cuba. They had only to check their equipment and their aliases. The money, carefully marked by Eduardo's wife, was passed out, along with the rubber gloves, Scotch tape, walkie-talkies, bugs and debuggers, a stamped addressed envelope containing a check to pay Eduardo's country club dues in case anybody should pass a mailbox, a map of suburban Washington tax delinquent property, cameras, more money flown up from Mexico for the occasion, a box of Preparation H, and a list of sterile phone numbers.

The plan was needlessly simple. Bill who is Al was to check into room 723 at the Howard Johnson Motel across the street from the Watergate. In case he was tailed by any of the McGoverns he was to order up a club sandwich with

two or three different flavors of ice cream, and then go to
the balcony, take out his binoculars (included) and pretend
to look for Democratic girls getting undressed. If inter-
rupted by the police, he was to explain that he was collect-
ing material for Commandante Eduardo's next spy novel
and refer them to Liddy and Hunt who would, meanwhile,
have checked into the Watergate Hotel where they would
be playing low-stake gin rummy. At the same time, McCord
would lead the Cuban real estate syndicate into the Watergate office building next to the hotel. The realtors would
enter through the basement, first picking the locks, and then
taping them, all the way up to the Democratic National
Committee offices. Simple. Dangerously so.

Now a digression. Critics of President Richard Nixon's
administration attack him most severely for his racial pol-
icies, his opposition to busing, his cutting back welfare and
food stamps and postal money orders. They point out that
there has not been one important black person in the whole
history of his conduct of the government. But that's not
true. One black man played a bigger role in the Nixon
administration than Henry Kissinger, the horny hampster
of cafe society and diplomacy. He is Frank Wills, the $80 a
week General Security Service guard at the Watergate.

"That's one goddamn nigger I wish we'd left *on* welfare,"
the recluse told H.R. (Bob) Haldeman one morning a few
days later as he sat in the White House dining room while
Manolo fed him his cottage cheese. "Remember that lib-
eral, that Pat Moynihan, we used to have around here, H.R.
Bob?" the President asked, "always wanting to put those
darkies to work. Well, you see what happens when you do.
Give one of 'em a job, and he'll do it. What I want to know,
H.R. Bob, is what happened to that old stereotype darky
that you could count on not being able to count on? Where
are those dear, old unreliables? Can you believe it? Here I
am, the cheese eating President of these United States, the
President of all the people, all the states, and I get caught

"Yeah, honey, I already picked up the laundry. . yeah. Okay, baby, fine. I just gotta check out one more thing here and then I'll be right home."

Saturday night by the only sober nigger in Washington. I tell you, H.R. Bob, these people aren't ready yet."

The facts of the fiasco are known. With McCord, the old CIA outer perimeter man, going ahead of the realtors, they made first penetration through the basement door about 2 a.m. and then, after taping the latch back, they picked, taped and picked locks up to the offices of the DNC. Gaining entrance to Larry O'Brien's office, they were groping for the fuse box at just the moment that Frank Wills was testing the basement door and ripping the tape off the lock. Upstairs they'd found the fuses, so McCord sent Bernardo out for beer.

On his way back with the beer, Bernardo sees the basement door is locked again and that somebody has ripped off the tape. Putting down the package with the three six packs, he picks the lock, retapes it and goes on upstairs where the guys are. "Who wants a brew?" he shouts, "and by the way, the next time one of you guys goes downstairs, please leave the tape on the lock."

"None of us went downstairs," McCord says.

"Well," Bernardo answers him, "it musta been the mailman."

McCord, the veteran CIA-FBI operative/agent, is on the walkie-talkie. "This is Unable Fox One, do you read me?"

"Read you? I can't even see you," the walkie talkie answers.

"Whozzat?" McCord wants to know and the walkie-talkie replies, "Can't you tell? It's Al. I mean it's Bill." McCord is slightly pissed, so he says, "You're not Bill on this mission, you're Base Unit. Roger and out." He puts down the walkie-talkie and starts out the door to go talk this over with Eduardo, and so he doesn't hear the walkie-talkie say, "Roger?????"

McCord gets over to the room at the Watergate Hotel just as Liddy is about to clean out Eduardo and explains the door situation. Liddy doesn't dare go back to the Big Boys without some very good poop. McCord returns to the offices of the DNC and tells the Cubans the mission is go. "We don't abort."

Down in the basement, Frank Wills has decided to abort the mission all by himself. Frank Wills has called the cops.

Metropolitan Police Sgt. Paul William Leerer in radio cruiser 727 "responded in front of the Watergate about seven car lengths from the main door." After getting a quick fill from Frank Wills, Sgt. Leerer said that, "We responded down to the area where the tape was found and after looking at the door we figured we had somebody inside at this time. We had a burglar going down on us. Myself and Officer Barrett and Officer Schoffler responded to the 8th floor by way of the stairwell. We found no other evidence of any tampering with any of the office doors leading off the main hallway on the 8th floor, so at the time we responded back out to the stairwell and while Officer Barrett responded to the 9th floor, Schoffler and myself responded down to the 7th floor."

It's a little difficult to picture but the boys in blue were getting close to the beer and real estate party in the DNC. Now to pick up the Sergeant's narrative: "We responded down to the 6th floor. The door leading from the stairwell had been taped in the same manner. I walked halfway back up to the 7th floor and yelled for Barrett. I said we have another door taped and responded come down here to assist us . . ."

Armed with nothing more than revolvers and one of the great all purpose verbs of all time, the DCPD in the person of Officer Schoffler and Sgt. Leerer went out on the 7th floor balcony outside the DNC's offices where one of them saw Al who is Bill across the street on his Howard Johnson Motel balcony looking through his binoculars and eating a three scoop ice cream cone. Al who is Bill decided on the basis of Officer Schoffler having his gun drawn and his being a boy that he probably would not turn out to be a

good-looking girl volunteer and maybe he'd better get on the walkie-talkie. "Unable Fox One," he shouted into the transmitter. "This is Al who is Bill and you better cool it or somebody's gonna get your foxy tail."

Static on the walkie-talkie and then, "You stay there and eat your ice cream. We're playing cards over here." Pause, and then Al who is Bill and who is getting worried says, "Sorry, I must have dialed a wrong number, but if you happen to run into Unable Fox One the blue hounds have just about got him treed."

Indeed they did. We were now only seconds away from the biggest bust since the French Connection. In the Sergeant's words, this is how the end came: "We responded in the area of the hallway and we met up again with Officer Barrett checking the offices that were open as we came down the hallway. We came into this room and I heard Officer Barrett yell, 'Hold it, come out.' At this time, I responded back out of the cubicle I was in, jumped up on the desk, and, drawing my weapon, when I looked over this glass partition there was five men standing in front of a desk with their hands either raised above their heads or at least shoulder high wearing blue surgical gloves."

At about the time Sgt. Leerer is making his last and biggest response of the evening, Al who is Bill hears Unable Fox One whisper into the walkie-talkie, "They got us," and then he hears a voice asking, "Are you gentlemen members of the Washington Police Department?"

Minutes later G. Gordon Liddy and Eduardo come running into the room. Eduardo is very upset, jumping up and down and screeching, "I gotta pee, I gotta pee." After he does, he comes out of the bathroom and screeches, "I gotta get a lawyer."

Next as Al who is Bill remembers it, "Eduardo removed a walkie-talkie, put it on the bed and told me to pack up everything. 'Get the hell out of here, get yourself the hell out of here, go somewhere. Go to Connecticut,' he told me.

He proceeded to go out the door to the elevator, but before he got in I asked him, 'Does this mean I don't get to go to the Convention in Miami?'"

*"Mr. Magruder, please . . . Jeb? Hi, this is
Jim McCord . . how's everything going out
in California? . . . Good, good . . . Nice
weather? . . . hey, that's great! No sense
being in California if it's not sunny . . . .
hee hee . . . right . . right. Say, Jeb, I'll tell
you why I called . . ."*

2. How We Just Drifted into it: A Peer Group Tragedy

"In this job I am not worried about my enemies. It is my friends that are keeping me awake nights."
                                             Warren Gamaliel Harding

Let's set the players on Saturday morning, June 17th, 1972. McCord and the real estate syndicators are in the hoosegow. Eduardo has vanished. Al who is Bill is sleeping it off in Connecticut. G. Gordon Liddy is having his mustachios waxed by Sally Harmony in CREEP headquarters. John W. Dean III is sleeping off jet lag in a San Francisco hotel. The Big Boys, John Mitchell and retinue, are in the Beverly Hills Hotel in Los Angeles. J. Daniel (Buzz) Ehrlichman is in the White House running the American Empire because H.R. Bob had to take the big cottage cheese to Florida to get him away from Brill.

Brill, first name and alias unknown, had been stationed by CREEP, at a cost of $45 a day, outside the White House in loin cloth and sandals with a sign reading FUCK YOU, NIXON – VOTE FOR MCGOVERN. Every time the boss looked out the window, there was Brill with his sign, and every time the boss would get angry and call the Secret Service to say, "Get that bum outta here." So Brill would be arrested, carted off and retrieved by a CREEP agent.

"That's our own guy," H.R. Bob would explain and Mr. President would simmer down for awhile until he saw the

37

sign and then he'd get mad all over again and have Brill arrested. H.R. Bob would then go over the whole thing again and explain how Brill was there to shock the long lines of optometrists with their Instamatics and their wives and children waiting to tour the White House Shrine. "Well, why can't you put an asterisk on the sign so it can say in small print he really doesn't mean it?" Mr. Pee would ask.

A compromise was needed so H.R. Bob arranged for a cabinet meeting — they hadn't had one in a year anyway — where it was agreed to double the size of the American military mission to Botswana and change the lettering on Brill's sign to NIXON SUCKS.

It was also decided to take Mr. President off to the Key Biscayne White House and have Ziegler announce he was on a "working vacation."

Now the play begins to get complicated. On Saturday morning, June 17th, G. Gordon Liddy, the General Counsel for CREEP's finance committee, tells his secretary, Sally Harmony, that his brush is shiny enough and calls Jeb Stuart Magruder, the Deputy Director of CREEP, who's having breakfast with eight or ten of the other Big Boys and their wives at the Beverly Hills. That in itself is something since Liddy had threatened to shoot Magruder a couple of months previously because Magruder had put his hand on Gordon's shoulder. Gordon is touchy.

As Magruder remembers it, Gordon says, "I should get to a secure phone and I indicated to him there was no way I could get to a secure phone. He indicated there had been a problem the night before. He indicated our security chief had been arrested at the Watergate, and I said, 'You mean McCord?' and he said yes. I think I blanched, to say the least, and said, 'I will call you back immediately on a pay phone to get more details.'"

It was sometime, however, before Magruder called Liddy back. Neither he nor the other Big Boys could come up with

any change. All they had in their pockets were one hundred dollar bills in consecutive serial numbers. But the word was spreading. Mrs. McCord called Robert Odle, Jr., the 28-year-old director of administration for CREEP, to say, "Jim has been involved in a project that's failed. He's in jail." It is not reported that Odle said, "Gee whizz, Mrs. McCord, that's too bad. What have they got him in for? Rape?" Spectacular incuriosity seems to have been the standard around CREEP. Like Robert Odle, Jr., Hugh W. Sloan, Jr., the 32-year-old kid out of Princeton, who functioned as campaign treasurer, kept right on walking that same morning when Liddy passed him in the hall and said, "My boys got caught." What boys? Got caught where?

Not everyone was dying of ennui. In the grand tradition of the CIA, the realtors had snipped the labels off their clothes and all other signs and tokens which might lead to their identification. They carried nothing but the tools of their trade and their address books, in which Eduardo's name was carefully written with the notation — "W. HOUSE." Operatives or counter agents from The Washington Post remarked on the entry, and began the difficult, painstaking detective work of finding out who this mysterious Eduardo might be.

They called the White House and asked for him.

Miss Cloverdine, the White House switchboard operator, said Eduardo wasn't in his office, but, yes indeedee, he certainly worked there. But while The Washington Post was trying to find him, Buzz Ehrlichman was trying to hide him. He had Miss Cloverdine put in a rather unpleasant call to Chuck Colson, yet another White House aide, who had hired Eduardo in the first place. "Get that Eduardo of yours on the first outbound jet," Buzz said and at the same time, H.R. Bob was on the phone to Jeb Stuart Magruder, the deputy campaign manager, suggesting that, "You get off that ass of yours and on the first inbound jet."

Thus began one of the less well known but more

exhilarating weeks in American history with all kinds of folks leaping on and leaping off planes at Andrews Air Force Base and Dulles International Airport. CREEP mobilized. As Bobby Odle, Jr., the administrator, said to the Senate Committee many months later, "Gosh, it was a wonderful week. Everybody worked hard. We kinda came together as a team that week at CREEP."

While an all-points bulletin went out to every law enforcement agency in the land that, under no circumstances were they to find out any more about the break-in, CREEP employees rushed back from leisurely weekends to man the shredders. But while there was an enormous expenditure of energy, considerable confusion existed over what was to be shredded.

The people at CREEP were ordered to go through the files and pick out *"politically sensitive material"* but they were to do it without reading it since it was all top secret, classified and documentary evidence of a conspiracy to break the law. Some Creepsters decided that, under the circumstances, it was more practical to shred the laws. If the laws were destroyed, there'd be no way to prove that they'd been violated.

So against the protests of the American Bar Association, they began stuffing copies of the U.S. Code and the Constitution down the shredders. Search and destroy missions combed the city for copies of the Ten Commandments. The Library of Congress was raided by a baby Creepster office boy who carted off the Code of Hammurabi and stuffed it into a fifth floor shredder. The overworked machine's reject button lit up and a repair man from IBM came over to explain that he'd have to send to Pittsburgh for special parts if they were going to feed it cuneiform.

The shredders were being worked 24 hours a day. The sixth floor shredder overheated and caught fire. It was discovered that a secretary had caused it by inserting the entire Bible instead of following instructions, which were to rip

41

out the Ten Commandments and return the unshredded portion to the church from which it had been taken. But Liddy, always the stickler, wanted the Sermon on the Mount shredded, too, while the folks in accounting objected on the grounds that shredder capacity — even with the new machines donated to the campaign by ITT —was being dangerously overtaxed.

Consulted on the WATS line, Billy Graham sided with the accounting department, and warned that if too many sections were excised from the Bible, even on national security grounds, there would be complaints. so the decision went against Liddy who retreated mumbling, "It's those little details that come back to haunt you."

Down the street in the White House, Ehrlichman was beginning to doubt the wisdom of shredding on such a scale. What if a Creepster was caught breaking into someone's house stealing the family Bible and the Constitution? It might be explained, but only with the cooperation of the Joint Chiefs of Staff and the Pope.

Ehrlichman had another approach and walking down the corridor to John W. Dean III's office, he found the Counsel to the President frantic and on his back under his desk with a flashlight. "I forgot the combination of my safe and I can't remember where I wrote it down," Dean explained.

"Forget *your* safe, it's Hunt's safe I'm worried about," said Ehrlichman taking hold of a foot and dragging Dean out from under. "But my honeymoon money, my honeymoon money's in the safe," moaned the younger man, who then cut himself short by remarking, "Besides, I don't think Hunt has an office here."

"Save that line for the FBI," said Ehrlichman, dragging The Honeymooner down to Hunt's office where they broke into his safe. Ehrlichman hauled out the contents and gave them to Dean with instructions to "deep six 'em."

"Whazzat mean?"

"When you're driving home to Virginia tonight, drop

that stuff in the Potomac and feed it to the fishes," the President's advisor for domestic affairs replied.

"Look, couldn't I please get that money and go on my honeymoon?" asked Dean. "Destroying evidence is work best left to the police. They're trained. They know how to do it."

"Okay, I'll call up L. Patrick Gray, III, and tell him — "

"Junior," interrupts Dean. "He's L. Patrick Gray, Jr."

"Well, he's also the head of the FBI," Ehrlichman answers in irritation. "He should be qualified to destroy evidence. In the meantime, you put this stuff in the trunk of your car and ride around with it."

By coincidence other people were putting other evidence in the trunks of their cars. CREEP administrator Robert Odle, Jr. was loading up as was Hugh W. Sloan, Jr., the campaign treasurer who was stuffing his automobile with $40,000 Finance Chairman Maurice (The Collector) Stans had ordered him to drive around with.

This brings us to the topic of money.

You'll be able to follow this discussion if you keep the distinctions in kinds of money in mind. First there is Old Campaign Law or pre-April 7, 1972 money, next there is New Law money. Of course, some 1972 campaign money is Old Law and some New Law, depending on who's auditing the books. In addition, there is Mexican money, Philippine money, dirty money, clean money and left over money which is the money they hadn't spent in the '68 campaign. Also, it's well to bear in mind there is secret money, hush money, slush money, cash money and Luxembourg money, but not too much of that.

Keeping these distinctions firmly in mind and not forgetting that you can get 8 per cent on 90-day U.S. Treasury bills, we should be able to follow where the money went. A lot of it was in Herbert W. Kalmbach's safe. Kalmbach was the President's personal lawyer and so was entitled to two safes, one in California and one in Washington where he

44

kept large sums of money, that is, some of it was Old Law money, some New Law, some secret, some hush, but none slush. When he gave $350,000 to Gordon Strachan, H.R. Bob's man, he was in effect converting hush to slush, which is permissible under the Internal Revenue Code, Section 315, but what's questionable was the further conversion of some of that money from slush to tush by placing it in Dean's safe where it served as a honeymoon credit line.

Certain other mixed moneys from Kalmbach's safe were invested in the San Clemente real estate investors syndicate on a leaseback arrangement so that the Kalmbach money was "made whole again" by placing 5.9 acres and the garage in a trust arrangement administered by the Orange County Community Chest and Bebe Rebozo. An IRS ruling was obtained certifying the trust's tax exempt status, thus permitting the issuance of $5,000,000 dollars worth of convertible debentures, 20 year straight term, on the Nixon Memorial Library and Rumpus Room, which permitted a pass through tax accelerated depreciation on the resultant investment leveraged by the trust debentures which were in turn underwritten by Chase Manhattan, sold in a string of Little Rock, Arkansas pawn shops and audited by Price, Watergate according to generally accepted principles of accountancy.

Some of these convertibles were placed in an escrow account at El Tio Pepe's French Custom Laundry and Dry Cleaners in Mexico City. A lot of hullabaloo has been made over this fact, but the truth is that John W. Dean, III, having remembered the combination of his safe and having married a New Orleans socialite and Ozark Airlines stewardess, had been honeymooning in Mexico City, when one morning, after an especially enjoyable party, he sent his wedding suit out to El Tio Pepe's to have it cleaned and pressed without removing the negotiable securities from his breast pocket.

It was in this accidental fashion that the slush money was

legally converted to tush money, not by Mexican laundering but by French dry cleaning. A more serious problem to funding the campaign was the IRS regulation that imposes a tax on political donations of more than $3,000. Thanks to this regulation, W. Clement Stone, III, Jr. (his father was W. Clement Stone III, Sr.), the Chicago insurance billionaire, suffered irreversible paralysis of his right hand.

In order to get around the $3,000 tax free limitation CREEP was forced to set up hundreds and hundreds of separate organizations, each of which a contributor could donate his three grand to without having to pay a tax. Thus were chartered Americans United for a Moral Society, Americans Not Yet United for a Moral Society, Billy Graham and Other Americans For a Just Peace Committee, The Society for the Preservation of High Priced Raw Milk, The Bob Hope POW Fund, the Ted Agnew/Responsible Leaders for Reform in Society Committee, Americans and Frank Sinatra for Civility, Americans and Others for American Airlines, The Ron Ziegler Committee for a Responsible Free Press, Americans for Peace with Honor in Viet Nam, Americans for Russian Wheat Sales, and so forth and to each W. Clement Stone, III, Jr., who wished to give $2,000,000 to the campaign, was required to write out a check.

As the word spread among other Nixon contributors that you'd get your arm broken if you didn't contribute or get it paralyzed if you did, it became obvious that some adjustments in the method of payment might be needed. The orthopedic surgeon in attendance on Mr. Stone gave it as his professional opinion that paralysis of the check writing hand might be avoided by the use of cash.

It was for medical reasons, then, that Robert Vesco put his $200,000 in New Law cash tush money tokas on tisch in the famous black attaché case. Much, much later, when Stans and Mitchell were indicted, it was alleged that the

"Listen, Sloan boy, my advice to you is to remember that when the going gets tough, the tough get going to, say, Mexico."

money was paid over to get them to influence the Securities and Exchange Commission which was suffering from some kind of obsessional delusion that Vesco had fraudulently made off with $224 million from ten thousand South American dentists and an equal number of Johannesburg Taco Bell franchisers. The evidence was so thinly circumstantial that nobody ever bothered to order Ziegler to deny the charge, and everybody at the White House was saddened when the chairman of the SEC was forced to resign, a victim of fiscal McCarthyism.

The only thing anybody's ever been able to make stick against Vesco is a charge of lese majeste. This revolves around his contribution of $350,000 to Jose Figueres, the President of Costa Rica, who wrote a letter to Nixon complaining that the SEC investigation would not help the dentists of South America but jeopardized Costa Rica's becoming "a showpiece of democratic development in the Western Hemisphere." It was felt in some patriotic circles that matters had come to a pretty pass when a Central American tinpot could command one hundred and fifty grand more than the President of the United States. It was this fact, according to a Marvin Kalb analysis on CBS, that caused Nixon to complain America had become a pitiful giant, and also got Kalb on the White House enemies list.

Now, to return to the developing conspiracy. It was showing signs of poor planning and lack of coordination. G. Gordon Liddy, who once ran for the House of Representatives from Duchess County, New York, with the slogan of SEND A CRIME FIGHTER TO CONGRESS, rushed to Burning Tree Country Club to complain to the Attorney General of the exuberant crime fighters who had jugged his boys, "Get the hell away from me," said Richard Kleindienst who was to display the same tin ear for nuance throughout the coming months, "Can't you see I'm playing golf? FORE!!!"

While the Attorney General shot through, and while ex-

49

G-man, ex-Assistant D.A. Liddy, who'd made a local name for himself as the guy who used to lead the weekly raids on Timothy Leary's Acid Manor Estates at Millbrook, discovered the accused have rights too, a key staff member at CREEP was manifesting a deficient aptitude for team play. Young Hugh W. Sloan, Jr., the campaign treasurer with two FBI agents parked outside his door, had decided matters were not proceeding as they'd been described to him in his poli sci course at Princeton.

At first, when corporate executives, followed by hit men, would come shaking up to his desk and unload briefcases full of boodle, often tipping the water carafe and dislodging the onyx ballpoint pen set given him by his father-in-law, the lad would tell himself that allowances had to be made for certain divergences between textbook and reality. Likewise, he chalked his surprise off to his own youth and inexperience when he asked Liddy to run downstairs to the bank on the first floor and cash one of those strange Mexican checks that were coming in and it took two months to get back the money, less $2,500 for a "cashing fee." It was remarkable that Mr. President had such strong support in Mexico, but then again, not really when you think about his kind of leadership.

Still, why did CREEP pay so many people in cash? Odd. Well, they're older and wiser men. There must be a good reason for them to tell him to sew up those stacks of bills in Mr. Mitchell's mattress, and stick the records in the shredder. But what could Mr. Stans have meant when the boy sent to him and asked why and had been told in reply, "I don't want to know and you don't want to know."

The FBI men in the vestibule wouldn't go away, so Sloan, whom the other kids at summer camp used to call Duke, got in to see John Mitchell. "I was essentially looking for guidance," is the way the young fella described it afterwards on national TV. "The campaign was literally at this point falling apart before your eyes, nobody was coming up with any answers as to what was really going on. I was essentially looking for guidance, at which point Mr. Mitchell told me when the going gets tough the tough get going."

So Sloan got going over to the White House where he saw Chapin, Mr. President's appointment secretary who told him to get a lawyer, and then he saw Buzz Ehrlichman who said, "I don't want to know and you don't want to know" and he should get a lawyer or go on vacation or how about a return to the private sector? Then they took him to a cocktail party on a yacht in the Potomac where Ehrlichman considered telling Dean to stuff him in with the contents of Eduardo's safe and deep-six Sloan along with the merchandise. There were no other Princeton graduates on the boat that night and all the White House Yale men could say was get a lawyer or go on vacation. Finally, docking at the Mariott Motel next to National Airport they stuck him in a room and wouldn't let him out except to march him on to the next plane to California.

California, however, isn't the automatic answer it used to be. They already had Martha there, locked up in Newport Beach, but it wasn't working. She had a knack for getting to the phone and dialing United Press International and saying, "I'm a political prisoner." Then they'd rush at her, take off her panties and jab a needle in her ass. She'd come to, phone UPI again and inform the world that, "They threw me down on the bed — five men did it — and stuck a needle in my behind. I'm black and blue. They left me in California with absolutely no information. They don't want me to talk."

Contacted back East, John Mitchell was quoted as saying, "She's great. That little sweetheart. Crunch. I love her so much. Crunch, crunch, and that's what counts. Crunch." Actually, though, John was falling into a funk so deep and bad he was about to quit the campaign. It wasn't fun any more. He couldn't help Bob Vesco and he couldn't help his friend F. Lee Bailey who had a client with a technical problem involving the Treasury and a boat load of gold bullion. Moreover, he was beginning to entertain doubts that many of the members of the team had a genuine talent for crime. They weren't living up to the promise they showed in spring training, which would have been alright except the whole administration was developing a serious problem of lower echelon zeal for law enforcement. He knew that H.R. Bob and Buzz both were constantly on the horn to L. Patrick Gray III telling him to rein in the troops, but his agents were still at it, questioning, getting bank records, and even threatening arrests.

Every time they'd get Gray III on the phone, which wasn't often because he insisted on spending his time "out in the field with the men" he'd say, "I'm trying to low key it. I've got it low keyed way down, but you wouldn't want me to do anything to disillusion the men, would you?" Soon they began to whisper around the White House that Gray III was showing signs of going native, that he'd taken to wearing a badge and had insisted on personally making a bust on a guy for transporting a stolen car across state lines.

"It's perfectly obvious," H.R. Bob said, "we have a cop problem on our hands. I'm going to have to talk to the boss." Knowing how touchy Mr. President was about preserving his deniability, H.R. Bob knew he would have to pick a time when the boss was feeling particularly mellow to discuss the alarming rise in FBI arrest statistics. Accordingly he chose a moment shortly after Mr. Pee had been fed his evening cottage cheese at the conclusion of a most productive work session with the Secret Service wherein it had been agreed that Brill would be able to make his point just as well, and the dignity of the presidency could be maintained if the sign was changed from NIXON SUCKS to NIXON EATS SHIT. "I think it suits my image better, don't you, H.R. Bob?"

The faithful German Shepherd thought that it did perhaps more justly reflect the positive aspect's of the Presi-

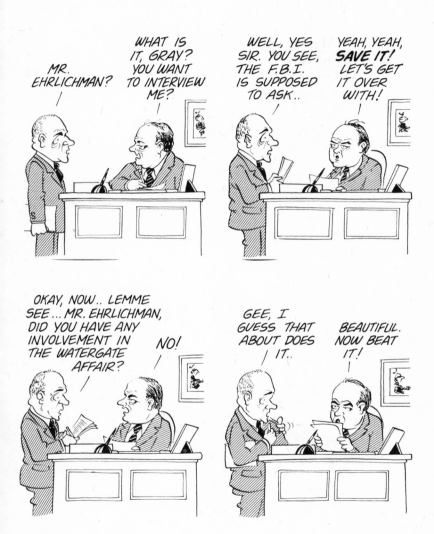

dent's program. He then began to describe L. Patrick Gray's unaccountable internalization of the role of the cop and had begun to go into detail when Nixon stopped him with a slow wag of an index finger and said, "I don't want to know and you don't want to know."

"But My President," H.R. Bob answered, "I know already and you gotta know sooner or later." Mr. President grew reflective at that, jotted some notes down on his legal pad, and then replied, "H.R. Bob, if I could choose any time in history, and if I could choose any place in the entire world, I'd want to be born right here in America today. That's another line for the marble on the Nixon Memorial, wouldn't you say so, H.R. Bob?"

"It's right up there with the New American Revolution, My President." Quiet in the Oval Office, and then, "You know, H.R. Bob, I've been thinking. Lincoln is sitting in his memorial and Jefferson is standing in his, so what does that leave me? Don't they have Adam floating on a cloud in the Sistine Chapel? Something like that might be good with a hand reaching down to inspire those who are to follow, but it could be interpreted as a subliminal pro-drug message, couldn't it?"

"No, not if they know it's you, My President."

"Well, well, we'll see. Leave me, H.R. Bob, I must be alone with my thoughts," said the Boss and H.R. Bob stole out to set up a meeting with L. Patrick Gray III, John W. Dean III and the archimandrites of stealth, the cowled abbots of the CIA, Richard Helms and General Vernon Walters, the Agency's Director and Deputy Director. H.R. Bob had an idea.

The archimandrites would be ordered to tell Gray that he must give up the investigation, especially the one centering around El Tio Pepe's French Custom Laundry and Dry Cleaners, because they were exposing the CIA's bolita business and putting their agents in jeopardy. Dean would be ordered to stop driving around with the contents of

Eduardo's safe and hand it over to Gray who would put it in an FBI burn bag and have it destroyed. If Sloan got back from his vacation without a lawyer they'd stick him in it, too.

Gray stuck the stuff from the safe in the burn bag, but complained that Sloan probably wouldn't fit. Even though they don't get their shirts done at El Tio Pepe's but at the Mandarin Chinese laundromat, the archimandrites said okay and told Gray he was messing up their bolita game, and Gray reluctantly said okay, but he wanted them to send him a memo on it for his files. The archimandrites weren't about to put anything in writing.

"But this is for national security," H.R. Bob said.

"Look," the archimandrites told him, "you can go to jail for national security around here. What if they find out about the national security golf carts at San Clemente? And the national security gazebo? And the national security ice maker and the national defense gardenias and internal security coffee table or the top secret rugs or the classified drapes or the executive privilege sofa or, god forbid, the constitutionally inappropriate beach house? You guys have to realize you may not win the next election, but we are career public servants, and the line between patriotism and embezzlement is thin."

With that the archimandrites rose from their chairs and, covering their fannies with asbestos pillows, departed thence to the monastery of espionage, their spy monkery, where they dictated memos concerning the meeting to their scribes and caused them to be placed in the files from which they were taken months later and given to the Senate. H.R. Bob was cast down, but not Gray. He was up and bouncing around the room, full of enthusiasm and getting good feelings touching the brushy top of his crew haircut with his fingertips. "I'm going to low key, just as you said, but I promise you, H.R. Bob, the FBI is going to push on with the investigation until we get to the bottom of it. Then you're

"Gentlemen, I think my statement was perfectly clear. I am leaving the campaign for personal reasons related to my family. So it's not what you think."

going to get the surprise of your life."

H.R. Bob listened to him, and he too touched the brushy top of *his* crewcut, but it didn't give him that good feeling, so he said, "No, you're going to get the surprise of *your* life when you finally get to the bottom of it and you have to place yourself under arrest."

"No, you're wrong. You just think we did it. The noogs did it. The McGoverns have got a double agent noog in here somewhere and he did it."

"What's a noog?" H.R. Bob asked, making a mental note that if he didn't get a haircut soon it would be long enough to pull.

"A noog is what the McGoverns call their goons. You know how they get everything bassackwards. They got noogs and guths that put up the signs and dress up like jocks to break up our meetings, and we got goons and thugs to pull down the signs and throw them out of the meetings."

H.R. Bob's mind flashed on Brill. Could he be a noog pretending to be a goon who is really a guth? Like Mitchell, the German Shepherd also felt nothing was going as it was supposed to. It was a helluva note, he reflected, that here they were in control over all the police departments, spy agencies, wire tappers and spooks, and the only crooks they can get arrested are themselves. He silently wondered if the Frondeurs who tried to overthrow Louis XIV were as fouled up as his gang. That was a conspiracy with a little dignity. Those guys probably weren't constantly tripping over each other, and neither, he thought, had Guy Fawkes. It was then he allowed himself one rare moment of disloyalty to Mr. President. What if they were caught? It could work out that he and not his President, would be accused of being the ring leader, the mastermind. Wouldn't that be something, the Guy Fawkes of America? Why June 17th might be made into an official legal holiday and named after him — H.R. Bob Day with bonfires, bells and little children going around taping the locks on doors. He saw now why it was important to keep the President out of this.

But as he was considering how, the Great Cottage Cheese came flying out of the Oval Office in a curdling rage. There had been a bureaucratic foul up and his instructions to the Secret Service concerning Brill hadn't been properly executed. "Look! Look!" the Chief Executive shouted, pointing out the window to Brill and his sign in Lafayette Park. In freshly painted letters, it read NIXON SUCKS SHIT.

"Mo: Bernstein and Woodward onto some-thing. The honeymoon is abort. At this point in time, I love you. John."

3. Scapegoat Time at San Clemente

"The trouble with Republicans is that when they get into trouble, they start acting like cannibals."

His Leadership, 1958

It was a good summer and fall. They won the election, set up a Committee for the Repeal of the No Third Term Amendment, and had enough money left over for John Dean to go on a honeymoon. So he married a blonde Castro Convertible sofa, had her upholstered in gold fleck, made four payments on her and relaxed with but one care in the world — the shortage of Grandpa's Wonder Soap. This is the soap he'd been using since he and Barry Goldwater, Jr. had been on the swimming team together at military school and his hair had started falling out. The exclusive use of Grandpa's Wonder Soap had arrested this unhappy development, and Dean's devotion to it was so great that it and a taste for Brooks Brothers clothes are his only known character traits.

Still, there were difficulties. A Young Republican from Cedarcrest, Ohio, who had been ordered to masquerade as a Gay Lib leader for McGovern, blew his cover in a Chilicothe fag bar by calling the morals squad when another customer gave him a pinch in the fanny. At an Ames, Iowa, Shriver rally, a gang of Mitchell/Magruder thugs and a gang of Colson/Chapin goons mistook each other for rival noogs and guths and were arrested for brawling in the streets. It was four days before the Republican sheriff could be persuaded to release that "gang of damn left-wing hippies." In California Roger Greaves (code name Sedan Chair I) resigned from his position as a leader of a Donald Segretti political sabotage ring, which would have been alright but he called a press conference and complained that the pay was low and the work was dull. His example inspired a young lady named Strumpet Foam who was employed in a San Francisco house of permissive repute to call the Governor of California and threaten to have a press conference of her own unless paid a large sum of money.

Eduardo, a more serious proposition, had taken to calling up Special Presidential Counsel Colson and making it clear that $12,000 a week was his base figure. So many people were popping up around the country and announcing that agents from CREEP, the Justice Department or the White House had attempted to recruit them to commit burglary, goonery or tomfoolery that Mr. Pee almost wished Brill was back in front of the White House instead of over in Foggy Bottom where he'd been transferred to carry around a sign saying BILL ROGERS GIVES GOOD HEAD. Instead, Mr. President ordered Dean to fold up his Castro Convertible and make an investigation, a real one whose results wouldn't be made public. Dean found out every member of the White House staff was secretly running his own string of operatives and that some of them had "run wild" to use the expression Mr. Mitchell employed when he dropped in to have breakfast at the White House and apologize for the confusion. His Leadership, who's a kind and forgiving man once you get to know him, said to forget it. But he was worried about the payments to Madame Binh to set up Dr. Kissinger, the President's personal international beaver shooter, in a Peking joss house. It was explained to him that the only pictures of the incident had been taken by a Russian satellite and that Brezhnev was willing to hand over the

DAVID, YOUR RECENT BOOK, "THE BEST AND THE BRIGHTEST" HAS REALLY TAKEN OFF! HOW DO YOU EXPLAIN IT?

I THINK, MERV, THAT THE QUESTIONS OF THE VIETNAM QUAGMIRE HAVE LED MANY PEOPLE TO BECOME CURIOUS ABOUT THESE BRILLIANT JOHNSON AND KENNEDY AIDES WHO FIRST GOT US INVOLVED OVER THERE.

WELL, I WOULD THINK THAT WOULD BODE WELL FOR YOUR NEXT BOOK, DAVID. AS I UNDERSTAND IT, RECENT EVENTS HAVE INSPIRED YOU TO START WORK ON A HOT NEW SEQUEL!

THAT'S RIGHT, MERV. IT'S CALLED "THE WORST AND THE STUPIDEST."

OH? WHAT'S IT ABOUT?

negatives and Henry's socks for seven million metric tons of soy beans.

The frazzle and hassle of all these foul-ups mainly came down on John Dean III's balding head. He'd secured a new supply of Grandpa's Wonder Soap, but he was expending it at an awful rate trying to iron out matters like the Washington cab driver who'd been employed as a courier to deliver documents between Muskie's Senate offices and his campaign headquarters. CREEP had bribed him to take pictures of the stuff and deliver the copies to them. The system had worked well until the Muskie campaign folded, but the cabbie had gotten used to the extra income and was coming around demanding more work or else. Dean was able to solve the problem by matching the driver's problem with Segretti's problem.

Segretti's problem was that the press and a couple of grand juries had learned that he was the head of one of the sabotage rings called Black Advance. It was imperative that Segretti go underground. The only operating underground network in the country was being run by fugitive Black Panthers and Weathermen, but Segretti said he didn't mind too much, he believed in being a good soldier in His Leadership's cause. However, after several weeks of living with the tackiest sorts of left revolutionaries, Segretti blew up and called Dean to say he couldn't take Bernardine Dohrn's constantly teasing him about his short hair. The solution was to load Segretti in the cab and keep on the move ahead of two process servers and an NBC news crew. Authorities in several Idaho communities received inquiries that summer about a strange Washington, D.C. taxi, plastered all over with Nixon bumper stickers, but since the cab wasn't soliciting fares in violation of local law no action was taken.

Making these kinds of arrangements took up so much of Dean's time it was often late at night before he got home to his Castro Convertible and then he was too tired to do much more than lie on it. He was also shut out of the list-making parties at the White House where senior staff would sit around and copy out the names of everybody they were going to screw after the election. Chuck Colson, who everyone acknowledged had the biggest hate on, used to call the parties political gang bangs or fucking without love.

Sometimes these parties would end in such awful fights that one of the aide de camps or Secret Service men in the hall would knock gently on the door and ask if there was something he could do to help. The fights were usually personal, like the evening Buzz Ehrlichman peeked at Magruder's list and saw his own name. Colson used to put everybody's name down but people were used to that kind of thing from him and paid no attention.

One night there was truly a terrible fight. It started when Mitchell was caught putting Ehrlichman's name down, which Buzz called a "cheap shot, John, a very cheap shot." John erased Buzz's name, but then he glowered his meanest stare at Ehrlichman, the one the doctors had always warned him against using on white men.

There was a silence for awhile until Colson told an aide to get him the Chicago phone directory. "I got my wallet picked in that town once," he said and began copying names. Mitchell got up to look over Colson's shoulder and he said, "You've got your grandmother on that list!"

"I'd kill my grandmother to help re-elect my president," Colson shot back, but Mitchell said, "Like hell, you would. You want her killed for her money, and you'll say you did it out of loyalty. That's a goddamn conflict of interest situation. You have your nerve pulling that in front of me, a former Attorney General of the United States. I ought to have you shot and thrown out the window."

"Nobody asked you," retorted Colson, "and look who's talking about conflict of interest! Mr. ITT himself." Soon they were standing nose to nose, and that's something, and screaming the names of corporations each said the other had been helping. They would have come to blows except

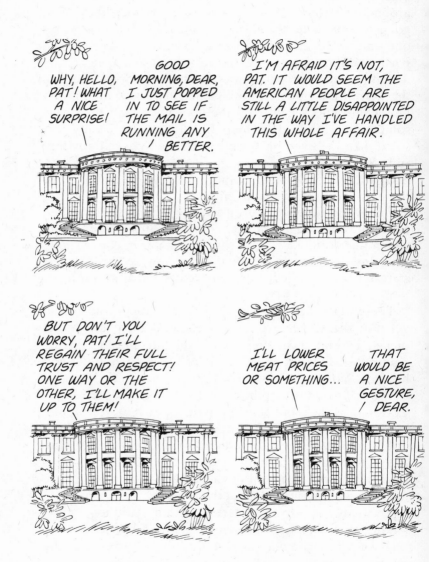

SCAPEGOAT TIME AT SAN CLEMENTE

H.R. Bob said it was time for everybody to give him the lists and pencils, and that because of the disagreements he was declaring all of the names inoperative. "From now on," he said, "there has to be unanimous consent before a name can be put on the list. It's more democratic that way, anyhow." They agreed and immediately voted to put all the black Congressmen on the list plus Bella Abzug.

More and more calls for money were coming in. Eduardo was eating it up by the bankful, and now there were the lawyers, expensive lawyers from firms like Alch and Yech, and the Wall Street partnership of Sharp, Sly, Slick & Slip. So it was decided to leak the existence of the lists. Rich radic libs, seeing their names left off, would pay good money to get on the list and avoid the stigma of being considered a friend of the administration. As an added consideration, those donating $5,000 or more were promised they would not be sent to a jail with criminals but would have a place in the camps with the real politicals. Pucci-Guccis and other sorts of radical chics giving more than $50,000 were also guaranteed a bunk next to a famous left wing scientist, artist or intellectual. Right wing richies were told what had happened to W. Clement Stone, III, Jr.'s hand and reminded of the trouble Bob Vesco had gotten into, and then it was explained to them that they could write one large check in any amount to buy their way onto the list without violating the Corrupt Practices Act. The money poured in but the lawyers took most of it.

Troubles were piling up faster than stolen votes in a Texas election. Eduardo was demanding ever more blackmail money and the costs for arranging perjury were going way over budget. Sharp, Sly, Slick and Slip explained they charged $400 an hour to coach truthful witnesses and $800 an hour for liars. Furthermore, since this is a specialized field of law, they needed to retain the firm of Grabby and Snatch as associate counsel. Their fees were so high that Mr. Pee had to get the money from Brezhnev but it cost him another million metric tons of soy beans and a five day bombing pause in Laos.

Moreover, some of the perjurers were not coming through. Sloan, the young Princetonian who served as CREEP's treasurer was way out of line. "You'll be a big man around the White House," Dean begged him. "I can guarantee you membership in the EOB (Executive Office Building) eating club, and a White House pass that'll let you cash bad checks in every bar from here to El Paso." But Sloan would only whine, "You can go to jail for that." Dean even promised him a varsity N for his sweater, but still Sloan said no, so Dean told him to take another vacation.

These were trying days for Dean. After a session with Sloan, he'd get a call from Segretti who'd be leaning out the back window of his Yellow cab talking from a pay phone on the I-98 bypass outside of Terre Haute. Always it would be the same question: "Alee-allee in free yet?" And always Dean would say, "I'll tell you when, and can't you find some place besides Terre Haute to drive around? There's a federal penitentiary there."

Some nights Dean wouldn't have the strength to pull out the Castro Convertible. He would rub a palm across the gold flecks of the upholstery and then fall into a troubled sleep in which he would review some new catastrophe like what had happened to John Caulfield, the ex-gumshoe from the NYPD red squad. John had been up on top of a ladder propped against a telephone pole in a driving rainstorm trying to tap Peter Malatesta's phone. Malatesta, an Agnew aide, as they say in the papers, was also Bob Hope's niece and was suspected of leaking like an old battery. The tap wasn't working because all they were getting was the Dow-Jones averages and Dial-a-prayer, so Caulfield had been pulled off his regular assignment of surveying the Kennedys' sex life to fix it. But up on top of the ladder with a flashlight, a set of tools and an instruction booklet, the unfortunate man had lost his balance and plummeted into a

Georgetown garbage can. The gin bottles and grapefruit rinds had broken his fall but he'd still dislocated a shoulder and was now demanding workman's compensation.

On the brighter side, Magruder and Bart Porter had, after a surprisingly few rehearsals, learned their lines well enough to be allowed to testify at the trial of Eduardo, Liddy and the realtors. Magruder had gotten Porter, who was the scheduling secretary at CREEP, to go along by telling him, as the little Creepster remembers it, that, "My name had been brought up as someone who could be counted on in the pinch, as a team player. My vanity was appealed to when I was told my name had come up in high counsels."

In fact, the poor little Porter was so far down on the table of organization that he was over on the next page of the flip chart. If they ever had, they ceased mentioning his name in high counsels when he got nailed for perjury. Cast off and abandoned by the big boys, he wailed into the national television cameras that, "This whole affair has had a most devastating effect on my personal life. Because of the unfavorable publicity, I have been terminated from a lucrative position in private industry, a fact which, in turn, has caused me to forfeit, at substantial loss, the purchase of a new home in California."

The Magruder-Porter perjuries were necessary, even at the risk of termination, because they were the logical ones to lie and conceal the fact that crime fighter Liddy had been given 200,000 fish to finance the Watergate real estate speculation. The money was to have been spent on buying the most up-to-date bugging equipment, but since the hardware had been supplied by the CIA it got Dean to thinking, and what he thought was that CREEP had been ripped off. He instructed Sharp, Sly, Slick & Slip (the case was handled by senior partner Elihu Sly himself) to institute suit for recovery but that blew up when they sent bailiffs over to serve writ of replevin and repossess Gordon's moustache.

Sally Harmony, better known in federal grand jury circles as the Georgia Forget-Me-Not, threw a scene and swore she would recover from her case of amnesia just in time to tell the Ervin Committee not only about the secret Gemstone files she'd typed, but also about Ruby I and Ruby II and possibly even about Crystal.

In the meantime, Mrs. Eduardo died in a great puff of $100 bills as her United Airline plane splattered short of the runway at Midway Airport, Chicago. United, unlike American Airlines, had failed to make a contribution and was experiencing a run of bad luck. Later on it was alleged that the plane had been brought down either by the Colson-Kalmbach faction or the Mitchell-Magruder clique. Enough credence was put in this fantasy that a late night emergency meeting was called in the EOB basement where H.R. Bob looked around the room at all His Leadership's advisors and asked, "Has any of you killed anybody lately?" By way of answer, a voice from the ring of men asked, "Does Wallace count as a kill?"

Shortly after that the trial started, and despite the fortune that had been handed over to Liddy, Eduardo and the spics, not one of those seven bastards would plead guilty. Clearly the time had come for a White House counter offensive. Colson was ordered to buy a double-truck ad for $16,000 in the New York Times, the text of which exposed the whole mess as a noog/guth plot, and gave the American people the choice of getting the MIA's back or pestering and distracting Mr. President in his pursuit of peace. The ad was signed "Welfare Mothers United and Vietnam Amputees for Nixon" followed by a list of the names of the last three months' winners of the New Jersey State Lottery.

After the ad came a full-scale rolling media barrage in which surrogates, deputies, cowboy movie stars and the ambassadors from the Warsaw Pact countries were sent on speaking tours crisscrossing the nation. The full impact of the major media push is best described by quoting from Pat

*"Heee's makin' a list, checkin' it twice!
Gonna find out who's naughty or nice. . ."*

Buchanan's News Digest. Buchanan, whose brother runs a Mexican laundry and dry cleaning business in Bethesda, Maryland, is hired to read all the newspapers and watch all the TV news shows and boil it down into a daily summary. This filter preserves His Leadership's serenity since it spares him the pain of looking at Jack Chancellor's ugly face but keeps him up to date on the broadcaster's slantings and twistings. Here follows a digest of the digest during the period of the media counter-attack:

UPI and AP carry unbiased story of Clark MacGregor Omaha speech quoting him as saying, "The Washington Post has maliciously sought to give the appearance of a direct connection between the White House and the Watergate." No mention made of this on either Chancellor or Cronkite, but the Smith-Reasoner show gives it eight and a half minutes . . . Gallup Poll reports 59 per cent of Americans approve your leadership . . . Harry Kawalski (your new Secretary of Commerce — you haven't met him yet) appears on the Dudley and Georgette Show (WCOW-TV, Birmingham, Ala.) and attacks elitist noogism . . . Harris Poll shows 56 per cent of electorate say they would vote for you again . . . All media give wide coverage to riot at Watergate 7 trial which breaks out when greaser defendants try to storm the bench and force Judge Sirica to put them in jail . . . E. Throckmorton Rogers (your new Secretary of the Interior — you haven't met him yet) appears on KASS-TV, Santa Ana, Calif. to defend you on local news shows. As a result of failure to watch the little red light on top of the camera is shown goosing the weather girl . . . Gallup Polls reports 51 per cent of Americans approve your leadership . . . All nets carry Ziegler statement accusing The Washington Post of "a shabby and a blatant effort at character assassination." Dow-Jones slumps to 800 and your leadership rating in latest Harris Poll is at 49 per cent . . . PBS (all stations on the network) carries charming Sander Vanocur piece on your dog (His name is Checkers II, Jr. and he is a cocker spaniel in case you're asked at your next press conference) . . . CBS announces no more instant analyses after your speeches — they say they'll get you later . . . Watergate prosecutor Earl Silbert issues statement saying refusal of remaining defendants to plead guilty is a miscarriage of justice and will result in a long and costly trial for the taxpayers at which it may be necessary to call witnesses . . . Pearl Butts (your new Secretary of Agriculture — you haven't met him (?) yet) tells Tallahasee, Fla. C. of C's that McG is real leader of the noogs which has been done in all prior elections. AP reports a standing ovation . . . Last remaining Watergaters found guilty, but Sirica is refusing to put them in jail . . . All media give this story big play along with statement by Melvin E. Laird (your old Secretary of Defense — you haven't met him yet) that it's judges like Sirica who are mollycoddling muggers, burglars and extortionists . . . You are down to 47 per cent approval in the Gallup which is two percent better than your Harris approval rating. The Dow is down to 700. A new approach is needed.

The dipping Dow had Wall Street in near panic, and if people weren't throwing themselves out of windows it was because you can't open the windows in those new buildings, but, while the brokers stood with their noses flattened up against the panes figuring out how to execute the avalanche of sell orders, they were muttering that if the averages lost another 200 points impeachment would be too good for him. "When it hits 500, get the noose," they said over luncheons of peanut butter sandwiches in the park.

The situation had deteriorated to the point that Colson, H.R. Bob and Buzz Ehrlichman decided the only way out was a Ziegler press briefing. They hated to do it because it took so many hours to rehearse the one-time Disneyland guide on the Jungle Cruise boat ride. Even the White House press corps had caught on to the Ziggy Ron and had started calling him Pinocchio because every time he opened his mouth his nose grew. Back of the blue curtain in front of which Zigglefritz gave his briefings in the White House

OKAY, STAFF, NOW'S THE TIME FOR US TO DO SOMETHING ABOUT THE PRESIDENT'S SAGGING SPIRITS!
R.N. CAN'T BE AN ACTIVIST PRESIDENT IF HE DOESN'T THINK HIS REMAINING TEAM IS STILL BEHIND HIM!
EVERYBODY READY?! LET'S MAKE THIS GOOD AND LOUD SO HE CAN HEAR IT UPSTAIRS!
GIVE ME AN "N"!
N!

SCAPEGOAT TIME AT SAN CLEMENTE

press room, Colson called him "the dummy" and Buzz Ehrlichman, ordinarily such a kind man, referred to him as
"splinterhead."

Nevertheless, they felt they would have to undergo the
tedium of preparing him to answer the questions of the hos-
tile press corps. So the three White House heavies marched
down to the Ziggy Ron's office where they found the President's press secretary examining a new shipment of Nixon
souvenir plates he was planning to sell the tourists who
come each day in such large and venerating numbers.
"Welcome aboard, folks," he said to the three, "my name is
Ron and I'll be your skipper down the rivers of adventure."

"Oh Jesus!" Colson moaned.

"As we pull away from the dock, note the alligators so
please keep your hands inside the boat."

"Shut up, Splinterhead, it's us," said Ehrlichman. "Save
that spiel for the press."

There was a tiny turned-up smile on the wooden head's
face with two dimples and something like a glitter in his
empty glass eyes as he said, "On the left the natives on the
bank have only one aim in life — and that is to get
'ahead*.'" (Footnote * pun)

"You know," Colson said to H.R. Bob, "sometimes I
think the dummy is making fun of us."

After hours of briefing, Zigglefritz was ready to meet the
wolves of the media, and stepping in front of the blue curtain, he announced that Mr. President had just told him
John W. Dean III had completed a thorough investigation
of the whole Watergate matter and had "concluded it was
Egil Krogh, Jr."

"But, but, but," the media beasts, the wolves of television
and the jackals of print, shouted, "that's not what you've
been telling us for months, Pinocchio." For a second the
Ziggy Ron looked confused, but Colson whispered through
a slit in the blue curtain, "Note the media natives and keep
your hands inside the boat."

With that the puppet was restored to his normally cheerful self and said, "The other statements that were made were based on information that was provided prior to those events which have been referred to in the President's statement today. Therefore, any comment which was made up until today or previously was based on that activity. This is the operative statement. The way to assess previous comments is to assess them on the basis that they were made on the information available at the time. The president refers to the fact there is new material; therefore, that is the operative statement. The others are inoperative."

More moans and howls with people shouting, "For Chrissakes, what's an Egil Krogh, Jr? Is it a bird or another code name?"

"Let me just say that in relation to the subject you've been asking about, specifically, the Egil Krogh situation, I am not really prepared today to be responsive in any detail to your questions based upon the same proposition or premise that I put to you the other day. At some point, we will be able to and intend to be more responsive to your questions."

"When in hell are you going to tell us what an Eagle Crow is?" a jackal asked, but Papa Geppetto's boy answered that, "I can only say that any comment — and there will be a time, I assure you, for this subject to be discussed and to be raised. I don't want to because I've taken the position I've taken in the briefings before and have done so sharply because the questions are addressed at matter such as that. I will simply say to you that, as I said before — and therefore this is a repeat of what I've said previously — anything that I offered here in response to a question was based on such Egil Krogh, Jr. that I had available to me to make a statement."

For several days after the briefing, it seemed to all hands in the White House that Ziegler had succeeded in distracting the country's attention from Watergate. Everybody

was talking about the Egil Krogh, Jr. On CBS Severeid remarked that it was an endangered species under the jurisdiction of the Department of Interior. Senator Proxmire of Wisconsin said he didn't know what it was, but it cost too much. Evans and Novak told their readers it was the lobbyists' code name for the Trans-Alaska pipe line, and Joe Alsop said that, although he wasn't absolutely sure about that, he had it on good authority that the Russians had a bigger one and we'd better get cracking. Pickets appeared in front of the White House urging all and sundry to SAVE BABY EAGLECOWS while Joe Kraft observed these startling revelations of what had been transpiring within the Bureau of Indian Affairs served to underscore the dangerous concentration of power in the executive branch. Jack Anderson startled the nation by announcing that one of his leg men, acting on a tip from the Missouri Highway Patrol, had caught one, and the fur industry promised not to make coats from their pelts.

Almost everybody in Washington was off on the trail of the Eagle Crow-Cow, Jr., except James W. McCord, Jr., the old CIA peeping tom. As a man of 54, he figured he still had ten or fifteen good working years in him even if he had lost his job as CREEP chief of security on account of Sgt. Leerer catching him up in the Democratic National Committee offices wearing a pair of surgical gloves. So he'd been going to see a vocational guidance counselor, but all they could come up with was the hope that he'd be taught a trade at the Federal Correctional Institution at Danbury. However, when Judge Sirica had sentenced the Cuban Real Estate dealers to 100 years in jail apiece, he hadn't said a word about vocational training. All he talked about was punishment, which got McCord thinking that an indefinite stay in the slammer might not be the rewarding and educationally enriching experience his five hippy children kept telling him it would be.

His misgivings grew when the catalogue he'd sent away

for arrived from the Federal Bureau of Prisons. The curriculum they were offering was much narrower than he had supposed . . . laundry management . . . license plate production engineering . . . dish sanitation procedures . . . applied geology (rock cracking). Unlike the California prison system where innumerable young men like Caryl Chessmen, Huey P. Newton and Eldridge Cleaver matriculated to take the writing course, the Federal Bureau of Prisons was indifferent to literature. On balance, McCord decided his career aspirations would be better served if he sold his shares to other members of the real estate syndicate and worked out different plans.

It was over the weekend that the St. Louis Post-Dispatch broke the story that Colson had ordered Tony Ulasewicz to firebomb the Smithsonian Institution to destroy evidence of the thousands of baby eaglecow bones CREEP had amassed there that McCord decided to write his famous letter to Judge Sirica. For some time previous to McCord's decision the White House had been cognizant of McCord's weakening resolve which they'd tried to strengthen by giving him stock options and telling him to go to the phone booth on Route 355 near the Blue Fountain Inn Motel every evening after the NBC Nightly News and wait for a call. There the phone would ring punctually and Tony Ulasewicz would say, "Don't take immunity when called before the grand jury. Plead guilty. One year is a long time. You will get executive clemency. Your family will be taken care of and when you get out you will be rehabilitated and a job will be found for you. Now wait five seconds for the beep tone and you will hear a personalized recorded message from Dr. Billy Graham." Some nights the message would be from other celebrities like Frank Sinatra and John Wayne but their words were always spiritual and patriotic.

Unhappily, because Ulasewicz was another ex-member of the NYPD with a passion for secrecy which approached

"Gee, Herb, I hate to bother you with this, but I've got an auto loan payment due soon. I wonder if you guys could send me $125,000 in cash by noon tomorrow, if you know what I mean."

sickness, he spoke his nightly piece to the phone booth on Route 355 through an electronic scrambler. McCord, all of whose equipment had been confiscated by the Ervin Committee, had no de-scrambler. After six weeks of going to the phone and listening to gibberish, the increasingly bitter McCord began to feel mocked and abandoned. His resolve to send the letter to Judge Sirica was reenforced.

The letter said that if the Judge wouldn't sentence him to a hundred years in jail, as he had the Cubans, McCord would tell how everybody had lied at the trial and how the Big Boys were really behind the crime. Still he hesitated. A man could get run over by a beer truck for sending letters like that, and then John Caulfield, Tony Ulasewicz's boss, called and said, "Listen, pal, I woulda rung ya up sooner, but I dislocated my shoulder in a touch football game during a law enforcement conference out at San Clemente, but I'm back in town now, and I'm tellin' ya our offer is good. You plead guilty and we'll rehabilitate you. You're not a hardened criminal. You're a first offender, and I'd be willing to tell the parole board I don't think you'd do it again."

"But you guys put me up to it," McCord answered. "Why don't you plead guilty and get rehabilitated and I'll tell the parole board I don't think you fellas would do it again."

Caulfield could see it was going to take a face to face meeting to bring McCord around, so he suggested they meet the next evening at the second overlook on the George Washington Parkway across the river from the city over in Virginia. "Isn't that a cruising place where known homosexuals frequent for the purpose of making illegal contact with each other?" McCord asked.

"Yea, it's a perfect cover," Caulfield replied.

Still, McCord was deeply suspicious. How could he trust an administration that had denuded Barry Goldwater's native deserts of the enormous herds of eaglecows which once roamed there? He could get hit by a beer truck on his way back from the Caulfield meeting. So McCord told his wife Dorothy that if he hadn't returned from the second overlook by ten o'clock, she should run out of the house and post the letter.

At the second overlook, McCord got out of his car, walked across the carpet of gay pansies and got into the front seat with Caulfield, who immediately told him, "The President's ability to govern is at stake. Another Teapot Dome Scandal is possible, and the government may fall. Everybody else is on track but you. You are not following the game plan. Get closer to your attorney. You seem to be pursuing your own course of action."

While they were talking they failed to notice they were being observed by two members of the vice squad from the Fairfax County Sheriff's office. "Hey, get a load of those two old fart fagolas," the one dick said to the other. "Let's run 'em in."

By the time McCord and Caulfield had established their identity as heterosexual White House agents on a special mission, it was ten thirty and Dorothy had sent the letter.

"You know, John, this is going to be awfully hard on my wife, E. R. "Joanne"."

4. Trout Fishing in the Reflecting Pool

"Liddy said he would never reveal any information in the course of any investigation even if it led to him. But if we were not satisfied with that assurance he said that, though he was opposed to suicide, if we would instruct him to be on any street corner at any time, he would be there and we could have him assassinated."

Fred LaRue

Some people were holding firm. Upon being dragged before the grand jury and asked why Segretti spent last summer in the back of a Yellow Cab, Dwight Chapin, Mr. President's appointment secretary, answered, "That's none of your concern. This is private enterprise." His Leadership said, "Let others wallow in Watergate; We are going to do our job," and a number of baby Creepsters who were still so young the scales on their backs hadn't hardened yet were going around the White House admonishing each other to put steel cups in their jock straps.

At home in Virginia, shampooing his Castro Convertible, John W. Dean III remembered, "The first time I heard of the 'Dean Report' was on the Big Two News at 6 o'clock . . . Here was the Mr. President of the United States reassuring the American people on the basis of a report that didn't exist." If it got out that there was no report, the fact that there were 199,000 eaglecow bones in the basement of the

Smithsonian could be blamed on him, and it would get out unless one of the fleet of Schlitz beer trucks H.R. Bob had cruising the streets found McCord and nailed him with gusto. This could be justified on the grounds that you only go around once and McCord, in an attempt to drink more than his fair share, was on his second swig.

McCord, a known and named Methodist, was eluding the beer trucks with the probable result that he would make it to the Ervin Committee hearings and trigger a parade of rat fink squealers. There were other discouraging signs. Not only was the Dow still dropping, but clergymen, even in such solid sunshine new majority Goldwater states as Arizona and Mississippi, were upping the confession-of-sin input in their sermons.

Then L. Patrick Gray III broke and ran for a Senate Committee where on the advice of his minister he admitted he'd destroyed the evidence. In mitigation he said he did it to be an example to the men under him and to smoke the noogs out. Even so, the situation could have been stabilized if the top White House Horribles had been able to get together and concoct a plan.

A meeting was called at which Mitchell, Colson, Dean, Stans, Buzz Ehrlichman, H.R. Bob and some of the others came, but it got nowhere because all of them were so preoccupied checking their machines to see that they were recording, they were too distracted to talk. When they were able to put a few words together, it invariably happened that somebody's apparatus began emitting beep-beeps signifying it was time to change a reel.

Under the pressure, some of them began to crack. Kalmbach, Mr. President's personal lawyer, commenced shouting at Buzz Ehrlichman, "I was your friend. I lent you $20,000. I was unthinking and loyal, and look at the trouble you've got me in! In my heart I know I'm not a criminal. I came to you and I said, 'Buzz, we're friends, your wife Ermintrude is friends with my wife Hepsibah, and your

oldest boy, Buzzy, Jr., is pals with my oldest boy, Herbie III, and your little girl Sandy is friends with my little girl Sandy —remember how we named them after each other? — and your little dog Inky used to love to smell my little dog Brownie best of all the dogs on the block until he knocked her up and I had to have her fixed.' Don't you remember when I came and said that to you and how you said that was right and that always since we left USC law school we have lived in the same subdivision together and how we always split fees and crapped on our clients together. Remember you said that?"

"That's not exactly how I recall it," said Buzz Ehrlichman, who'd noticed that Herbie's batteries had run down and was moving in on the electronic kill.

"Buzz," Herbie continued to shout, "I know that Loyal Order of Elks button in your lapel is a microphone, but I'm saying what I have to say anyway. You can doctor the tape all you want. I want to know, don't you remember how I came to you and I said all that about Ermintrude and Hepsibah, and Buzzy Jr. and Herbie III, and the two adorable little Sandies, and Inky and Brownie, how I said, 'Buzz look me in the eyes, look me in the eyes and tell me if I become your bagman I won't get caught'. Didn't I say that? Look me in the eyes. Look me in my warm brown, endearing eyes, and you took your cold, gray-blue eyes and you looked me in my warm eyes and you said, 'You won't get caught.' So now I look you in your eyes, Buzz, and I say to you at this point in time, I ask you, Buzz, what are you going to say to me now?"

"You got caught."

For a moment it was so quiet in the Lincoln Room of the White House all you could hear was the gentle whirr of tape recorders and Fred LaRue, the millionaire Mississippi errand boy, sniffling and saying, "I'm guilty, I'm guilty, I'm guilty." The rest moved in on him in a tight circle, pushing their coat lapels out to ensure high fidelity recording.

88

H.R. Bob was unhappy. The team was coming apart before his very eyes. It was obvious that such dissension could lead to rat finkery on a mammouth coast-to-coast network scale with the result that Mr. President himself would be inculpated. Should that happen, H.R. Bob saw himself demoted in the history books to being a figure of secondary or even tertiary importance.

A few of the Horribles were even giving some thought to sneaking around H.R. Bob and going in to discuss the situation with Mr. President himself, but really there was no way of accomplishing it. Any telephone call to Mr. President was screened by H.R. Bob, and every call to H.R. Bob was screened by a young fellow named Strachan and his calls, in turn, were screened by G. Gordon Liddy who was in jail, and to reach him you had to go through H.R. Bob which was impossible. It was rumored that Mr. President was bugging himself, so that, as a consequence, a lot of people began looking around for counsel.

Always a Washington growth industry, lawyering spurted forward so briskly that the Chief Justice told the young men who come to him for career advice that in terms of profitability, the law business was every bit as good as trading in soy bean futures. "Watergate," the Chief Justice announced, perhaps a trifle too grandly, "will be for the members of the bar what the discovery of the Alaskan oil fields was to the energy industry." Expanding on the theme the white-haired, fatherly jurist declared, "I'm bullish on America."

As he spoke, government officials and businessmen predicted a shortage of bulls, steers, cows and heifers. "The only bull presently enjoying an oversupply is the kind that the American housewife will refuse to eat," they said. "The era of cheap, plentiful food is at an end."

The disappearance of the beef steak, that symbol of American strength and manliness, put the whole country in an ugly mood. Man-on-the-street interviews quoted people

89

as saying, "With the devalued dollar I can't afford to go to Europe this summer, and with the revalued yen, I can't afford to take my family to see America first in one of those neat Jap cars, so I'm going to spend my vacation watching Senator Sam hang the Horribles up by their ears on my crappy American-made black and white TV set."

The Horribles retained more lawyers to whom they expressed shock that the charitable dispensation of a million dollars to a small group of Cuban refugees from Castro's dictatorship should be regarded as a felony. The lawyers made sympathetic noises to their clients and discreet inquiries to the district attorney about immunity. The team was coming apart, but the most awful damage was being done by that committee with its wipe-out TV ratings. The numbers were so impressive that Ocean Oil announced it was cancelling "its sponsorship of Skylab and the Moon shot to bring you gavel to gavel coverage of Senator Sam and His North Carolina Jug Band. Ten thousand local Ocean Oil dealers, the company that never waters its oil or oils your waters, take great pleasure in making it possible for all NBC viewers to see these historic hearings. We are especially proud to bring you today's hearings which will feature as the star witness, R. Leekie Tanker, Jr., Chairman of the Board of Ocean Oil. In his prepared statement to the committee, Mr. Tanker will explain why he illegally donated $200,000 with the best wishes of your local Ocean Oil dealer. And here comes Senator Sam with his now famous Cherokee gavel."

Sam: We're right glad to have you here today, Mr. Tanker. I see you've brought your charming wife and distinguished counsel, which you are entitled to do because it is your constitutional right to try to make a good impression.

Mr. Tanker: I'd like to thank the chairman and explain that on the advice of counsel and after reviewing all the evidence against me, I'm accompanied here today by my public relations man.

Sam: Fine, fine 'cause the Fourth Amendment provides for an innocent man to be represented by counsel and the Fifth Amendment says a guilty man may remain silent while the Sixth specifies that a very guilty man may have the services of a flack at all times.

Mr. Tanker: The Ocean Oil Company is only guilty of supporting Mr. President and poor judgment. How were we to know it was to come out in the open? It has never come out in the open before. We relied on these men's promises, and they failed us. We were betrayed by bad advisors. We were stupid but not crooked as any one of our four million credit card holders will tell you. Incidentally, Mr. Chairman, our credit card is good for the purchase of tires and batteries also. Also, Mr. Chairman, we were given to understand that our contribution or fee, as we like to call it, was necessary to permit us to merge with Great Lakes Petroleum, a step that would have permitted us to complete our great dealer network and put us in a position to lay down an oil slick on both coasts and every major inland body of water. Furthermore, we are sponsoring this program and thereby aiding Senator Baker to get the Republican nomination next time. So in closing, I can only say that if Senator Baker is elected that he will give favorable consideration to a merger with Great Lakes Petroleum.

Sam: We thank you kindly for that statement. And now Senator Montoya will begin the questionin'. We always begin with him and then build up to the hard questions.

Senator Montoya: Thank you, Mr. Chairman. Now, Mr. Tanker, you are a great self-made businessman, and a credit to your family, I understand from reading the papers, so what I want to ask you, as an Ocean Oil credit card holder is how I can get my account straightened out. I pay my bill but your computer won't give me credit.

Mr. Tanker: You're talking to the right man, Senator.

Senator Montoya: I'm sincerely glad to hear that because

*"Ah am not bein' harassin' toward the wit-
ness, Senator Gurney. Ah am bein' gruff
and lovable and yew know it!"*

I have written you many times and attempted to call you by phone but have never been able to reach you. If you can take care of this mix up I shall advise my constituents with similar problems that you will take care of the difficulty under threat of a subpoena and a contempt citation.

Mr. Tanker: That's absolutely correct, Senator.

Senator Montoya: Well, my credit card number is A-275-1184. No further questions.

Sam: Now doesn't it say in the Book of Psalms, Number 26, the 9th verse, "Gather not my soul with sinners, nor my life with oily men: In whose hands is mischief, and their right hand is full of bribes." Doesn't it say that? 'Deed it does.

Ocean Oil sales spurted and other major corporations sent their board chairmen in to testify while their companies bid up the price of commercials so high the networks were getting almost as much for the hearings as for pro football. CBS petitioned the Senate to move the sessions to the evening prime time hours while Atlantic Records announced it had signed Senator Sam and the North Carolina Jug Band to cut an LP on the strength of the 45 hit sensation, "Dickie Dick Dick, You Little Bugger, You." Magruder, Colson and Strachan formed the nucleus of a rock group called The Horribles and were immediately signed up by MGM. Stax and Motown got into a bidding match that didn't stop until it had hit seven figures for exclusive contract rights for Jay Wesley Dean and the Castro Convertibles. Even Sally Harmony, G. Gordon Liddy's doobie-doobie-do girl, was invited on to the Carson show. Albert Grossman, the great rock impressario, said he would soon finalize plans for a Watergate Festival to be held in the bottom of the Grand Canyon. A four-day affair at which more than a million people were expected, it would open with a special ICBM fly by, but the biggest coup was the announcement by Clive Davis of CBS records of the purchase of the White House Tapes for two million dollars plus the exclusive use by the executive branch of America's ten most beautiful hookers.

Atlantic Records immediately sued CBS alleging the tapes were material originally discovered and developed by Senator Sam and his North Carolina Jug Band. Even with the White House words and lyrics in litigation, Senator Sam was zooming up to the top of the charts and playing to ever larger SRO audiences at Washington's most exclusive boite, the Caucus Room located high atop Capitol Hill. Variety was shouting SAMBILLIES BOFFO MONDO SMASHO ON NETS – IN PERSON!!!

Even in the Effete East Sambilly music was on all the juke boxes and the White House was getting scared. Obviously, something had to be done, especially with the new controversy developing over Mr. President's two faithful German Shepherds, H.R. Bob and Ehrlichman. The Democrats were demanding that they be put away, and even Senator Buckley and the Goldwaterites were saying that they would have to be wormed and given distemper shots. The Ziggy Ron issued a statement saying Mr. President would never treat his two loyal animals that way, and besides, the law gives every dog one free bite. That ignited a disgraceful press room shouting match with Peter Lisagor of the Chicago Daily News.

The Pentagon said they took the legal maxim to mean one free bite out of each person, and even though the Secretary of Defense swore he would take the case to the American people if necessary, it was apparent to all administration supporters that their side was losing ground rapidly. A counterattack was needed so Tony Ulasewicz was dispatched to Morganton, North Carolina, with a coin changer strapped to his belt so he would be able to phone his reports in without arousing suspicion by trying to break one hundred dollar bills at McGhee's General Merchandise and Dry Goods Store.

The redoubtable ex-flatfoot from the Bronx had as his

mission digging something bad up on Senator Sam back in his home town. Tony had made a name for himself paying off Mrs. Eduardo by dropping the cookies in airport lockers. He was the White House's most effective operative, but this assignment was murder on him. A lot of time was lost establishing the fact there was no Morganton stop on the BMT, and there was the problem of disguising himself so's not to cause talk. To this end, Tony took off his white-on-white tie, turned his diamond ring palmside and spent long hours at the American Legion post with an RC Cola always in hand while the young farm kids fed coins into the machine and danced to the Watergate Wallow, the Jug Band's latest hit. Tony pretended to enjoy the words along with everybody else. (Come on an' do the Watergate Wallow, everybody's doin' it, It's so easy to follow/you can do it pretty mean, much like John Dean/Or you can do it wrong like Gordon Strachan, Or you can do it in fits, jus' like Ulasewicz, 'cause everybody from your alderman up to Bob Haldeman except Dick Nixon, is fixin' to dance the Watergate Wallow.)

To throw off suspicion he changed his name and learned, at the price of throwing out a hip, how to do the new dance step. Little else of value did he learn. Uncle Ephraim Swink told him a lot about Senator Sam, but the only potentially damaging information Tony was able to pick up from these conversations was that in 1917 Senator Sam had fought on the same side as the French and the Japanese. He thought he might have stumbled on to something when he found out that in order to cut expenses during his campaigns, Senator Sam would sometimes share a room in the Raleigh Quality Court Motel with his entire staff, who was a big young tobacco farmer named Rufus. Did Uncle Ephraim Swink or Job Hicks think this was possible pederasty, Tony asked. No, both Uncle Ephraim and Job thought the new insecticides had pretty much got the pederasty along with the nematodes.

It was with this meager intelligence that Tony Ulasewicz returned to the nation's capitol. "An Alger Hiss, I would say as a former professional p'lice officer, this guy probably is not. I checked his farm out real good and was able to determine that the subject has a lotta pumpkins. Returning at night with my Scout knife, I personally examined the contents of each of his pumpkins, some 413 by count, and was able to determine that they contained seeds, pulp and what you might call glop, but no papers of any sort," Tony reported to H.R. Bob, "an' as far as the sex angle goes, well again, speakin', Mr. H.R. Bob, as a former professional p'lice officer, I would have to tell youse, that we are not confronted here with a Teddy Kennedy type individual. I was able to locate two witnesses that are willing to give us affadavits they seen the subject on a bridge, very, very early in the morning, but only for the purposes of tryin' to hook some catfish. At that point I had to break off my investigation and hot foot it for the Continental Trailways bus depot on accounta the Morganton Weekly Advocate and Citizen, which is the local rag there, had whatcha call a front page story on me sayin' I was a 'perverted pumpkin picker' being as they said, which is not a truthful or accurate statement of the facts, that I get my jollies from 'slashing gourds and tubers by night' an' also stating that an individual person known to cut up 413 pumpkins wit' out makin' 'em into jack o' lanterns or pies could possibly go after the cucumbers next an' is a proven menace to de community."

With nothing more to report to Mr. President than that some members of the Morganton First Presbyterian Church thought that Senator Sam read the Song of Solomon with perceptively more verve than either Kings I or II, there was no choice but to find some other target to focus the counter attack on. But what or who? A suitable victim had to be selected in a hurry for the Dow had dropped below 600 and dangerous clusters of Congressmen and stock brokers could be seen assembling on the street cor-

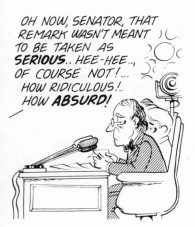

*"Mrs. Dean? There's a long distance call
for you from Vogue."*

ners. Cries of impeachment were shouted from time to time but most of the hostility centered on the two German Shepherds who were widely believed to be suffering from a fatal case of magnetic tapeworms.

H.R. Bob was getting freaked, so Mr. Pee, exercising his leadership role, tried to calm him by saying, *"We've had our Cambodias before."* But this was one more element that depressed the faithful major domo. Past experience showed the small-country-invasion crisis was an exhausted ploy, so instead, they rang up Big Pink on the hot line and asked him if he'd come over and try to get people's minds off the scandal. In due course, Big Pink arrived, the price of food went up and the Dow Jones went down as America got drunk, paid no attention and danced the Wallow. "H.R. Bob, I think I've come to my Seventh Crisis," Mr. President said. "Now the way I've handled these fiery tests of the soul in the past is that after I'm attacked, and my situation looks lost and bleak, Manolo and I retire with my yellow legal-sized writing tablets where in a condition of perfect withdrawal I don't sleep but purify myself through meditation. My concentration is so intense I eat nothing, not a spoonful of cottage cheese. When I have worked myself up into an overwrought, sleepless frenzy the DECISION comes to me in the form of a VISION, after which I fall on the floor in a stupor, but when I awake I am fresh, my will to strike back at my enemies has been tempered into frozen steel, and I return to the world with a terrible vengeful resolve to carry the DECISION out. So now I must go off to Camp David and undergo my spiritual ordeal."

Mr. President went chop, chop, chopping off to Camp David in his helicopter and endured his spiritual trial but when it came time for the Decision Vision, the voice did not speak as it had during Alger Hiss and Checkers and the Kitchen Debate and the other three crises. "Dick," the sepulchral voice of the Decision Vision said, "I don't think I can do much for you this time. This is a toughie."

"Listen, Decision Vision, at least you could call me Mr. President," the leader of the American people complained, and then added, "Why don't I fast some more and go sleepless another day, and maybe by that time you'll have thought of something?"

"Okay, I'll give it a whirl," the Decision Vision replied, "but don't get your hopes up. I'm not the genie in the lamp, you know. You're asking a lot from a figment of your disordered mind."

Accordingly Mr. President sat in his chair and neither slept nor ate so he could give the Decision Vision more time to think up a way out. He didn't know that the Decision Vision had become an envious self-hating spirit who felt that his master didn't give him enough credit. As the Decision Vision saw it, not only was his work unappreciated, but his master basically resented him, questioned his motives and presumed he was wrong without ever giving him the benefit of the doubt. Although the Decision Vision had been with him longer than anybody, except possibly Murray Chotiner, he was given no recognition for his loyalty, so now it was time to pay the master back for his ingratitude.

"Well, I gotta couple of ideas, Dick," the Decision Vision began malevolently. "First you gotta pass a law making it illegal for anybody to write or speak your name. That's what's demeaning and weakening the office. They say, 'President Nixon and they go 'yghaa!' But if they only say 'The President' and never connect your name with it, they'll have new respect for the institution."

"What's that going to do to my place in history?" Mr. President wanted to know.

The Decision Vision would have liked to say, "It'll cut you down to size," but he knew he couldn't, so he said, "Dick, you'll still have all the perks, the trumpeters and the fanfares, and the houses, it'll just be that folks will think more about your office and less about your (he wanted to say ugly) face, and that will enhance your prestige and

HOLY MOLY, CAMPERS! TIME FOR ANOTHER **WBBY** "**WATERGATE PROFILE**"! TODAY'S COVER-UP CUTIE IS... **JOHN EHRLICHMAN!**

"**JOHN EHRLICHMAN**, THE PRESIDENT'S ADVISOR ON DOMESTIC AFFAIRS, HAS FOR FOUR YEARS BEEN A CONSIDERABLE POWER IN THE WHITE HOUSE. YET UNTIL RECENTLY, MANY AMERICANS WERE UNAWARE OF THE SCOPE OF HIS DUTIES!

"ON THE AVERAGE DAY JOHN EHRLICHMAN USED TO CONSULT WITH MR. NIXON AT LEAST ONCE OR TWICE. IF THE WORD CAME DOWN HE WAS NEEDED, HE'D MAKE HIS WAY UP TO THE OVAL OFFICE WHERE HE WOULD INVARIABLY ENCOUNTER FELLOW STAFFER H.R. HALDEMAN!"

HALT! STOP OR I'LL SHOOT!

BOB! IT'S ME! IT'S ME!

popularity."

"Well, if you think so, Decision Vision."

"I do," said the tricky, self-hating spirit, and then he gave the vulnerable chief executive the worst piece of advice of all. "The kraut dogs must go to the pound. Buzz and H.R. Bob must be put to sleep, because the American people love you; it's your advisors they don't trust."

Upon President Truthful's return to Washington from Camp David he called the ASPCA to have them lead H.R. Bob and Buzz away. Without the two lightning rods for the growing popular hatred, the Decision Vision had left him defenseless with no one to advise him and carry out his orders but Dr. Kissinger, the German Gerbil, the Ziggy Ron and Manolo who had little to offer but cottage cheese and backrubs.

Again the Dow declined. Impeachment was spoken of openly. The mobs grew louder and more menacing. The Gerbil alternated between trying to figure out who might succeed Mr. President and how to establish secret relations with him and making valiantly inept attempts to save his boss on whom he depended for his power and his girl friends. "Let us not indulge in an orgy of recriminations," he declared, and when this pleading was received with laughter he took another tack in a major policy address at the annual banquet of the United Chiropodists of America. "The President's power to conduct foreign relations is being jeopardized by this Watergate Wallow of yours," he said, and then he pulled a State Department cable from his pocket as he told his audience, "To illustrate the strain this scandal has put on our diplomacy, let me read this wire to you, 'ALL CHINA NAUSEATED STOP SEND PANDAS BACK SOONEST STOP SIGNED MAO TSE-TUNG.' "

Nothing worked. The garden party for the POW's which Zigglefritz had gone to such pains to arrange had no effect whatsoever. The search for a third daughter in order to stage another White House wedding was a failure, while the

104

two extant daughters, in their first recorded act of rebellion against paternal authority defiantly refused to become pregnant. There would be no White House birthing or christening.

Bereft of H.R. Bob, Mr. Pee began to deteriorate. He would dawdle over breakfast staring at the black headlines in The Washington Post — NIXON CAUGHT IN SELF BUG ATTEMPT — or he would wander down to the Oval Office and idly play back old tapes of conversations he'd had with Buzz and H.R. Bob in the glory days of Phase I and Kent State. When Manolo would come in to inquire if next year's Federal budget was ready yet, he'd look up slowly and say in a lifeless tone, "I'm a winner, Manny, and don't you ever forget it."

The remnants of the White House staff were increasingly worried. Henry, the Tacky Teuton, decided that, *"Vot he needs is a zummit. De air vould be goot for him."* Several were arranged but no leaders from first, second or even third class powers would accept. They had to settle for a series of shabby rendezvous with prime ministers from under-developed countries whose principle exports were copra, bananas and the cheapest sort of au pair girls. A slightly classier meeting was pulled together with an oil rich emir from some principality in the Persian Gulf but the effect was pretty much spoiled by having to meet on the isle of Elba.

After his triumphant return, Mr. Pee announced gas prices would go up. The Dow immediately went down and the House of Representatives voted a Committee of Impeachment. The IRS then seized San Clemente in a gesture meant to forestall a Congressional investigation. Bebe Rebozo demanded that Mr. Pee either pay for Key Biscayne or give it back. Cordon Bleu Caterers, Inc. attached his bank account for nonpayment of the bill for the POW party, and then Norman Vincent Peale announced he was accepting an invitation to conduct a prayer breakfast at the

new Democratic National Committee headquarters in the Airline Pilot's Association building. The entire Republican Congressional leadership said they would attend whether invited or not. Bob Hope declined a White House brunch invitation citing a prior conflicting engagement to hit the first ball at the Frank Sinatra Pro Am-All Am-Chrysler-Coca Cola Golf Tournament.

When the House Committee voted a bill of impeachment out on to the floor, all the Splinterhead could think of was to suggest that Mr. President catch a bad chest cold and go to the hospital. Manolo agreed and it was decided to go ahead since Henry was unreachable with his phone turned off in an Odessa beach resort with a Soviet movie star. "Okay, I'll go," Mr. President agreed, but you're still lookin' at a winner, Manny, don't you ever forget it."

Surprisingly, although the political experts had predicted clear sailing for the bill of impeachment, it was running into serious opposition on the House floor. Many Congressmen rose from their seats to say, "Mr. Speaker, while I wish to go on record as favoring this bill's objective, I believe that impeachment would imperil national unity and tend to bring the Presidency itself into derogation. If the present incumbent is impeached, it is unlikely that many Americans will regard his successor as infallible, a state of mind that is hardly conducive to orderly democratic government."

The Senate, always more daring in such matters, voted to impeach, which meant the bill would have to go to a joint House-Senate Conference Committee to iron out the differences. Once in conference, the friends of the White House believed they could keep the matter bottled up for years and so notified Bethesda Naval Hospital. "Let's go home," Mr. Pee said to Manolo on receipt of the news, adding, "Didn't I tell you I was a winner, Manny?"

The stalemate caused the Dow to drop below 500 and Washington was quickly inundated by mobs of infuriated

Wall Street stock jobbers, investment bankers and bond salesmen. Every member of Congress was being hit by thousands of letters and telegrams demanding that they "throw the bum out." George Gallup issued a statement saying that for the first time in the history of his celebrated public opinion poll, a president had registered a minus approval rating.

After weeks of debate a compromise was reached. Mr. Pee would not be impeached. He would, in an act that Congress felt would bring us together again, be hung. The whole affair would be tastefully handled beginning with a signing ceremony at the White House where Mr. Pee would give away pens to the Congressional leaders, after which there would be a picture taking session in the Rose Garden and a short statement in which the chief executive would point out that this bill was a record breaking first. Pat Buchanan in his news digest reported that media response was little short of terrific.

A month after the signing would come the ceremony itself. It would take at least that long for the Pendulation Day Committee to reassemble the million dollar Inauguration Day glass-enclosed, heated reviewing stand where the gibbet would be placed, according to Willard Marriott and Bebe Rebozo, the two chairmen. The souvenir manufacturers needed the time to produce a sufficient supply of pennants, balloons, plates, noose replicas and little leaden gibbets with thermometers in them. The Postal Service began a crash effort for a commemorative stamp, and it was announced that the rope would be a Cherokee noose made by the same tribe that presented Senator Sam with his gavel. Ten thousand $100 tickets for the fifteen Pendulation Balls were sold within a matter of hours.

When the day came, the throng that had come to watch was too large to estimate. The city was decorated in red, white and blue, band music was in the air, and at the Sans Souci, Washington's most expensive restaurant, the dessert

"Simple, country lawyer, my ass!"

menu featured Impeach Melba.

At the appointed hour, Manolo helped Mr. Pee on with his burgundy dinner jacket and for the last time the leader looked out of the Oval Office window. His eye moved with approval across the reviewing stand where the diplomatic corps was seated next to the Justices of the Supreme Court, but then it picked up an infuriating image. Brill there with his last sign: NIXON IS WELL HUNG.

The Marine Band was blowing its fanfare preparatory to Hail to the Chief, when Mr. President wheeled and shouted at Ziegler, "I will not be pendulated in the presence of that sign." Everybody in the room explained with the huge crowd it would be impossible to get to Brill and arrest him. "In that case, I'm walking out the back door over to the Watergate. I'll be standing in front of the entrance just opposite the Howard Johnson's with my back to the street. You phone H.R. Bob and tell him that. He'll know what to do."

With that Mr. President adjusted his black bow tie, put his champagne glass down and, without saying goodbye to Pat or the girls, without giving splinterhead an affectionate rub, walked out the door.

A few minutes later, in another part of town, H.R. Bob climbed in behind the wheel of a 1937, four door, black LaSalle. Inside the car with him was Mitchell, Buzz Ehrlichman, and Kalmbach. Outside, on the running boards, each holding a Thompson submachine gun, were Dean and Colson.

H.R. Bob slowly put the LaSalle in gear. As it moved down the street a Yellow taxi turned the corner and Segretti, seeing the others pull away, leaned forward and shouted, "Follow that car!"

Notes

Notes

Notes

Notes

Notes

Notes

Notes